THE
SPATCHCOCK
PLAN

THE SPATCHCOCK PLAN

A COMMANDER SHAW NOVEL

Philip McCutchan

Hodder & Stoughton

LONDON SYDNEY AUCKLAND TORONTO

British Library Cataloguing in Publication Data

McCutchan, Philip
  The Spatchcock plan.
  I. Title
  823'.914 [F]

  ISBN 0-340-51338-1

Published by Hodder and Stoughton,
a division of Hodder and Stoughton Ltd,
Mill Road, Dunton Green, Sevenoaks, Kent TN13 2YA.
Editorial Office: 47 Bedford Square, London WC1B 3DP.

Photoset by E.P.L. BookSet, Upper Norwood, London.

Printed in Great Britain by St Edmundsbury Press Ltd,
Bury St Edmunds, Suffolk.

THE SPATCHCOCK PLAN

1

The incident had been reported by a semi-observant motorist simply because there had been so many similar happenings on motorways. It might have been nothing more than an argument, or it might have been something serious and criminal. The motorist, a middle-aged estate agent driving west on the M4, had seen a car stopped on the hard shoulder and some two hundred yards farther along there had been a van stopped by an emergency telephone and two men had been seen with a woman and there had appeared to be some dispute.

That was all.

No, he hadn't noted any registration numbers. He believed the car to have been a Metro and he thought it was a sort of dark red. The van had been a white Ford Escort, a somewhat dated model. No, he couldn't possibly identify the woman or the men, though he fancied the latter could have been from a Middle Eastern country; his impression was of olive skins. It didn't help much. The motorist had left the motorway by the next exit, Number 17, and hadn't reported what he'd seen until he'd got to Chippenham, by which time it was somewhat too late. However, the motorway patrols had been active and an abandoned Metro had been found. It was not dark red, it was dark green, but it was more or less where the motorist had reported seeing it, and it was suffering from a failed petrol pump, so the police settled for having found the right one. There was no sign of the Escort van nor of any persons in the vicinity. There was no immediate identification in the car of the Metro's supposed woman driver; she had evidently taken her handbag with her to the emergency telephone. But a check with Swansea would reveal all. The motorway patrol noted no evidence of any disturbance near the telephone, no blood-stains, no fragments of torn clothing. A check with police communications showed that the telephone had not been used at all that evening. Whoever had intended using it just hadn't made it in time before the Escort van pulled in. Some chancer, or chancers in this case, had struck lucky.

It was in the early hours of next morning that my security line burred in my ear. I woke at once although I'd turned in late. It was Max on the line – Big Max, Executive Head of 6D2 London, speaking from his penthouse suite in Focal House. His deep voice rumbled at me.

He came quickly to the point. "Bad news, Shaw. Miss Mandrake's disappeared – "

"Felicity!" All feeling of sleep had gone now.

"When did you last see her, Shaw?"

"Sixish, last evening – "

"Going where?"

"Cardiff. To visit an aunt."

"I see. She was hooked off the M4. You'd better get here, Shaw." Max cut the call and I sat on the edge of the bed for a moment, bewildered, looking at Felicity's things around the room, things she hadn't needed to pack for the overnight stay. Just a duty visit, duty familywise, nothing to do with her job as one of 6D2's top agents. Taking a grip on myself I dressed fast and went down to get my car out from the underground parking lot beneath the block of flats. My mind roved as I went fast for the City and Focal House: I knew the dangers of motorways to women on their own. Stop on the hard shoulder and you were asking for it, but of course there were times when a stop was forced on you . . . at this stage I didn't even know Felicity Mandrake had stopped on any hard shoulder, but the inference was obvious enough since you couldn't be hooked off whilst in motion. I thought of more obviousnesses: rape, murder. But in Felicity's case, not necessarily. She and I both made enemies, dangerous ones, in our professional duties for 6D2. On the other hand, it didn't seem too likely that a

8

professional enemy would have happened to be cruising past just when she'd broken down or whatever. Too much coincidence.

At Focal House I checked in with the duty guard. No matter that I was well known to him: our strict routines held and I produced my ID card. I was let through to the lift where I pressed the button for the penthouse suite, where Max had not only his office and that of his personal secretary but also a dining-room for entertaining VIPs and an opulent bedroom for when he needed to be on hand day and night. I went up fast past the various layers of the organisation: Foreign Office Liaison, Police Liaison, ditto CIA, FBI, Interpol . . . fingerprints, micro-files, translators and linguists . . . 6D2 was big and world-wide except for the Eastern Bloc, having tacit international backing from the Western governments even though we never worked overtly for them – we were in the background, fully trusted and well informed, and the fact that we were independent of all governments gave us an immense advantage in that we could often bend the law and, just so long as we kept officialdom out of it, get away with things that a bureaucracy could not. But all that had its dangers and now I was face to face with one of them.

In his palatial office Max said, "You'd better have a brandy. You look as though you need it." He pushed a decanter and a glass across towards me and I took a biggish slug; I needed it all right. As it went down Max told me what he knew: it was little enough.

"I gather the Metro was a self-drive hire car. DVLC Swansea put the police onto the hire firm. They passed on the name of the driver: Miss Mandrake."

"The TR7 was being serviced," I said, "and the aunt had a birthday lunch tomorrow. Today," I added. "What do you think this is, Max? A chance motorway pick-up, or what?"

He shrugged his massive shoulders, hunching himself like a bear. "I go for a chance, Shaw. Not her usual car – I doubt if she was being followed or anything like that. However, because of who she is, and because that estate agent reported seeing olive skins, I've put out an alert. All ports and airfields

9

are being watched. I've fixed things with the Home Office and Interpol. All that can be done, will be done." He added, "If this is a kidnap, someone's going to contact us. That's all I can say just now."

"And no-one's contacted."

"Early days," Max said. "Give them time."

Time, I thought – time for anything to happen to Felicity. The wait was going to be hell but currently there was nothing else for it. Like Max, all the signs seemed to me to point towards that chance attack, such as was becoming the norm, almost, on our motorway network. If you were a lone woman . . . my earlier thoughts repeated. Some nutter would be cruising past on spec and not too many passing drivers would be going slow enough to take much note. I felt my fists clench impotently; I wanted another brandy but I wasn't going to have one; I would be needing a clear head and maybe an ability to drive. I told Max I would go down to look at the files, see if anything jelled in my mind, some adversary from the more recent past who might have a need to kidnap Felicity for what might be gained from it. Max repeated that if it was a kidnap, Focal House would be contacted soon enough, but he realised my need to keep my mind occupied.

I went down to the computer section; I wasn't seeing what I was looking at. I kept seeing Felicity at some nutter's mercy, probably dead already and her body concealed in some undergrowth somewhere farther on along the motorway. Max had said the police were carrying out a search – routine, he said, that was all. Nothing had been reported, no finds. Max was being very decent about it all; I'd always known he disapproved of male and female agents getting emotionally involved but I'd told him, not exactly in so many words but he got the drift, to mind his own business. Felicity and I worked well enough together to nip his criticisms in the bud so he didn't press it. But currently I believe he was thinking that he'd lost two agents to one chance shot: I wouldn't be much use to 6D2 with Felicity on my mind.

And I didn't find anything in the files that helped. When breakfast time came I had a cup of strong coffee and a cigarette in the canteen and then just hung around HQ waiting for news, either from a possible kidnapper or the police to say they'd found the body.

After the second cup of coffee I'd steadied up a little and was beginning to think more coherently and constructively. I would go and see the car hire people, and for what it was worth I would talk to that estate agent from Chippenham. Something might emerge that the police hadn't managed to dig out. I was about to call Max when my bleep called me instead to the suite, and I went up at once in the lift.

"No time wasted," Max told me. "We were so wrong: this wasn't a chancer. It's a kidnap."

I felt my throat go dry. "They've contacted?"

Max nodded.

"Who is it, Max."

He said, "Remember Al Kufra?"

"*Al Kufra!*" Why hadn't I ticked over? It had been quite a while ago and the discs had been a bit of a blur before my eyes but I should have checked farther back and concentrated better. However, as it had happened nothing had been lost. Al Kufra came right back to me. A Libyan, known to us simply as Al Kufra, Kufra being the name of a group of oases in the Libyan desert. Al Kufra had been a kind of king pin around that part, and he'd carried out all kinds of overseas killings on behalf of his government until he'd been stopped in his tracks by 6D2, taken after an attempt to blow up an airliner at Heathrow five years or so before. Felicity Mandrake herself had been behind the arrest and Al Kufra was currently in a British jail, maximum security and life sentence.

"It looks like revenge," Max said. "An eye for an eye. But overridingly they want Al Kufra out. Until they get him, Miss Mandrake remains a hostage."

I took it in. After a while I asked, "Is there a deadline, Max?"

"There is. We have a week from the time of the call. If the British Government hasn't arranged the handover by that time, Miss Mandrake's body will be found in a place yet to be notified."

11

So I had a week. Just a week. Max had told me the telephone call had come from persons calling themselves the Friends of Al Kufra. The caller had been a woman. There was no indication as to the standing of the Friends of Al Kufra, whether or not they had the backing of their government in Tripoli, but Max believed that they would have, though this would remain in the background. Governments didn't normally blackmail one another openly.

I had precisely nothing to go on; I'd not been involved myself in the pursuit and arrest of Al Kufra – that had been Felicity's own assignment. I'd been on a job in South America at the time. So I didn't see this kidnap as an attempt to lure me into the net, chasing the bait that was Felicity. I saw it as it had been presented: sheer hostage work, and Al Kufra the only one who could save Felicity. Or rather, the British Government who would have to release him.

I'd asked Max about that. "Are they likely to concede?" I asked, knowing the answer, knowing what it would have to be.

Max said, "I can't speak for the PM, of course. But I don't see any concessions. I'll be talking to the Home Secretary soon and I'll let you know the reaction."

I'd had to be content with that. It was out of my hands, of course; and in the meantime there was plenty to get on with. How had the kidnappers got onto Felicity's car to start with, how had they happened to be right there when the car broke down? If it hadn't broken down so conveniently, what would they have done? Followed her right through to Cardiff and the aunt's house, which was in Llandaff – Cardiff Road, not far from Churchill's Hotel, a quiet neighbourhood apart from its traffic, not the best setting for a kidnap.

I went to see the car hire people. The firm was Regius Hire, in Kensington High Street. The boss was a man named Higgins and he remembered Miss Mandrake taking the Metro away the day before. He'd already told the police that, he said unnecessarily. She had given her address as c/o Focal House, as I knew she would have done; 6D2 agents never use their private addresses, for obvious reasons.

I asked Higgins about the petrol pump. He was sensitive on

the point. "Full service before the lady took it out," he said. "Nothing wrong then. Course, petrol pumps are funny, I dare say you know that."

I agreed that they could be funny. I asked about the mechanic who'd done the service. Higgins said he hadn't reported for work yet. A good hand, he said, reliable. He hadn't been long on the payroll but he'd proved his worth.

"Name?" I asked.

"Ibrahim," he said. "Comes from somewhere around the Mediterranean."

"Libya?"

"Could be."

He could indeed be, I thought. Something seemed to have been established. Ibrahim could have fixed that pump, I supposed, to pack up after around seventy or eighty miles – he could have picked up Felicity's route in conversation with the office staff – and he could have passed on the make and registration number of the hired car. It could fit. I said I would hang around a while; but when it became obvious that Ibrahim had no intention of reporting for work I felt that my prognostications had been confirmed and I got the mechanic's home address from the boss. I set off for an address in Stepney, knowing the attempt had to be made but feeling pretty sure Ibrahim would have flown the nest. Which he had. No-one in the building knew, or would admit to knowing, anyone by the name of Ibrahim or anyone who worked for a car hire firm in Kensington. It was a needle in a haystack, but I left a telephone number and a message about a reward.

Back in my flat, Max came on the security line.

"I've spoken to the Home Secretary, Shaw. Whitehall will take no action. They prefer to stand clear. For so long as the kidnappers play it this way, it's being left up to us."

"That means me," I said.

He came back on that fast. "Not so. You're too close to – events."

I answered him steadily. "I insist, Max. I want to do it. Felicity and I . . . we've worked together a long time, and

13

worked well. I understand what makes her tick. We have a rapport. I'm the one to handle this – believe me."

Max was still doubtful, but I pressed the point hard and I won out. Max gave a sigh and said, "Very well, then. Of course, you'll have all the assistance you need if you ask for it."

I said, "Just leave it with me for the present, Max."

"Play it low?"

"Play it my way," I said, "and for now anyway, yes, that does mean low."

He asked if I had any leads. I said, "Not really. Just a long shot that probably won't come off, but you never know your luck, do you?"

After Max had cut the call, I sat and waited for another ring that if it came would come on my ordinary outside line. The Ibrahims of this world are not noticeably loyal to anyone in particular, or some of them aren't, those who are not fanatics for a cause, and this Ibrahim just might be swayed by cash even if he took it from two hands at once, as it were. It had been known, and I'd dropped the hint that a large sum of money could be earned for information received. I sat and waited for a long time and tried not to think about what Felicity might be going through while I sat in safe comfort.

At just after 4 p.m. the outside line burred. I answered. "Yes?" I said.

A woman's voice, accented, said, "Who is this, please?"

"A man of money. Who are you?"

"A friend of Ibrahim. How much money, please?"

I said, "A hundred, to start with."

"You will meet me with the money, please."

"I'll meet you in the open and alone," I said. "Let's say, in Millbank. Outside the Tate Gallery. In one hour's time."

2

I didn't really expect too much; someone might be about to grass on this Ibrahim, or alternatively they might be about to pass false information and pocket the money. That was a chance I had to take, making a spot assessment when the meeting took place. The caller had said she was dark, tall and slim. She would be carrying a copy of a woman's magazine, *Best.* I left the flat and went by tube to Pimlico and walked through to Millbank. It was a fine afternoon, warm and sunny, and there were the usual hordes of tourists around. I went past the RAMC headquarters building, drifting with the crowd towards the Tate Gallery. I was early; I wanted to identify the woman caller, if possible, as she arrived and began to wait. I wanted to have a good long look at her before I made the contact, try to sum her up before she reacted to my presence. I didn't doubt she would turn up as arranged, otherwise why bother to ring, but I was surprised at the big risk she was taking. I could haul her in for intensive questioning and maybe I would. On the other hand she could have the thing rigged and I could find myself mugged and bundled into the back of a car. Doubtful, outside the Tate, but still a risk.

I waited on the river side, moving up and down. I looked at my watch: it was now just an hour since the call. Crowds moved past me, past the Tate Gallery across the road. The traffic was heavy and noisy, London beginning its homeward rush. Ten more minutes went by, and I crossed the road at a set of lights. There seemed to be plenty of tall, dark, slim women of varying ages and pigments but they were all on the move, and mostly accompanied. Then I saw the one with a

15

woman's magazine, coming from the direction of Parliament Square, and I saw the title, *Best,* held up across the woman's body.

I went towards her, casually, and our eyes met.

I said, "Ibrahim?"

"Ibrahim, yes. Where shall we talk?"

I said, "Here's as good as anywhere." I took her arm, and we walked on, past the RAMC HQ. She was dark, as she'd said, but not too dark, could be Egyptian, or Libyan. She was pretty, or had been, but now the prettiness was marred. A deep scar ran from the corner of her mouth up to her right eye, a knife gash, white and ugly.

She asked, "What do you want with Ibrahim, please?"

"I want to talk to him," I said.

"What about?" She turned her head and looked at me hard; I tried not to stare. There was something appealing about the girl – she was little more than that, and I felt sorry about the scar.

I said, "The matter's private. Do you know where he is?"

She nodded. "Yes, I know. The money, please?"

I brought out five tens, ready in my pocketed hand, and passed them to her. She riffled through the notes and said, "You promised a hundred."

"The other fifty will follow when I've talked to Ibrahim. Perhaps more. So where is he?"

She said, "You cannot talk to him. Who are you, please?"

"Someone who wants to talk to Ibrahim," I said patiently. "I think he can help me. If he will. Or perhaps you can. How well do you know Ibrahim?"

"Very well, for a long time."

There was something in her voice, a give-away. I asked tentatively, "Boy-friend?"

"Yes," she said. Then I saw she was crying, very quietly. "Ibrahim was a good man, with bad friends."

"Was?"

"Ibrahim is dead," she said.

*

16

I nabbed a taxi after it had dropped its military-looking fare at the RAMC building. We went to Birdcage Walk and into St James's Park where we sat on a bench and watched the antics of the ducks. I got the scenario: Ibrahim Suwesi had worked genuinely at Regius Hire as a mechanic. He was hard-working, a young man who had wanted no trouble in life, just to make his way peacefully and one day marry the girl. He had been no Libyan activist, but he had been made a cat's paw by certain of his countrymen in London for no good purpose. The girl, of course, didn't know the details about the Metro and its doctored petrol pump, but I could work those out for myself without much difficulty. Libya always kept tabs on its nationals overseas, especially in London, and Ibrahim's movements and employment would have been known. I remembered Felicity had made the hire arrangements with Regius in person at their office. She could have been seen by someone whose business it was to recognise her, and the chance sighting had been made use of, the innocent Ibrahim being pressured into co-operation. I asked the girl if she knew anything about the Friends of Al Kufra; she said she didn't, and I believed her. I don't think there was any duplicity about her at all. She had responded to my hints dropped at Ibrahim's lodgings simply because she had been distraught and had felt obscurely that the interested visitor might perhaps know something about Ibrahim's killers: also because she was short of money. Ibrahim had been keeping her, she said; and because of her scar she found it hard to get work. People shied away from her. It had been Ibrahim's brother in Libya who had knifed her because she had preferred Ibrahim to himself, and because his brother had been responsible for the disfigurement Ibrahim had never turned away from her as others did. Now Ibrahim was dead.

I asked her how it had happened, and if she could put the finger on the killers.

"I do not know them," she said. "They came from nowhere, and they took him away. Then a message came to say he was dead. The body, they said, would never be found."

They were probably right, I thought. There were so many

ways: burning, blocks of concrete, shredding, iron bars chained to corpses thrown into rivers to list a few. And Ibrahim the cat's paw had been safer dead once he'd played his part for the activists, the Friends of Al Kufra who had got Felicity in their grip.

I asked, "Aren't you worried now about your own safety?"

"I do not worry now," she answered in a low voice. "Without Ibrahim I have no life." She fingered the scar. I saw what she meant. But I wondered why it was that Ibrahim's killers hadn't made a clean sweep. After all, Ibrahim might have been supposed to have talked to her. I could only assume that they had a use for her, but I had no idea what it might be. I asked who it was that had passed on my message about a reward.

"One of the persons you spoke to," she said. "A man called Alef Wali, an Egyptian."

"A friend of Ibrahim?"

"Yes, a friend."

"Perhaps I could talk to him."

"Perhaps, yes."

There was no time like the present. I came up with another cliché: strike while the iron's hot. I was very much aware of time passing towards that deadline, though past experience did show that deadlines were fairly elastic. It all depended on how it was played, especially by the side under threat. If the British Government, say, could be persuaded to emerge from the shadows and look like playing along, we might gain a little time. For diplomacy read duplicity and nine times out of ten you'd not be far off the beam. Anyway, Alef Wali might be worth contacting and I decided to make the attempt right away since currently I had nothing at all to go on except maybe the Egyptian. I asked the girl if she would take me to him.

"Yes," she said. I passed over the other half of the reward and she thanked me. She looked a little diffident about it – it was, after all, a kind of blood money, profit made from the dead Ibrahim's misfortune, but when you're at the bottom of the heap you can't afford to be too particular. We got up from the bench and moved through thinning crowds of duck lovers towards Birdcage Walk and it was just as we reached the edge of the park that I became aware of the tail, a woman. I saw her make a not very well covered signal to a big black car with tinted windows waiting in the carriageway and then I saw a man lowering a window in the back of the car and I saw the snout of a machine pistol. I flung myself on the girl, bringing her down to the ground, but it was too late. The man was very fast. The girl's head shattered and a good many uninvolved people died as well in the spread of bullets, or so I was told later. Lead had given me a snick across my forehead and I'd gone out like a light. I was also told later that the car had made a clean getaway. There had been a lot of panic, not surprisingly. And of course there hadn't been any police around.

"You said a woman gave a signal to the car." Max disobeyed all hospital regulations and lit one of his expensive, hand-made cigarettes that he got from the Burlington Arcade. Admittedly I was in a private room, with a strong police guard outside.

I said, "Right."

"Libyan."

"That was my guess."

"Recognise her again?"

"No," I said. "Nothing outstanding, and the glance was quick."

"Nobody else seems to have been aware of her."

"They had other things to think about when the firing started."

Max nodded and blew smoke. "I understand there's no lasting damage to you, Shaw. Just an overnight precaution."

"Yes. I'll be out when the consultant comes round. So they tell me."

"And then?"

I said, "Alef Wali, the Egyptian. But I don't think I'll go to him."

"Very wise," Max said gruffly. "I'll have him brought in."

19

"Discreetly?"

"Discreetly," he said, and got to his feet. "Report in yourself when they release you, Shaw. We've got Whitehall on our backs and I'd like you to have a word with the Home Secretary."

The Home Secretary was Humphrey Bason, who sat for a very comfortable constituency in the south – Worthing West. He had about the biggest majority in the whole country. He was a comfortable man, fat, round and jolly, but I didn't believe he had much on top – I'd met him a few times and although he was always very nice and amiable he didn't strike me as a man of decision. He was more a man of procrastination and he liked to keep in with everybody. It was said that the Commissioner of Metropolitan Police made rings round him whenever necessary.

I met Humphrey Bason in the Focal House suite later that morning. His jollity was not very evident; he was a worried man that day, very worried.

"Of course," he said, "there can be no question of a release, absolutely none at all."

"Oh, of course," Max said smoothly. "That's understood, naturally."

"I'm so glad you see it our way," Bason said with obvious relief: he'd been briskly briefed by the Prime Minister, of course. "The PM's adamant, you know. Quite adamant. Al Kufra – a ruffian of the first degree, all those actual and potential deaths. We're very sorry about your Miss Mandrake, that goes without saying."

Max said, "You realise they'll carry out their threat, Home Secretary. They always do."

"Oh yes. I say again, we're really very sorry. What do you propose to do about it?"

Max spread his hands wide and shrugged. "Whatever we're told to do."

"Ah. By whom?" Humphrey Bason's chins wobbled a little.

"By you, Home Secretary." Max was very bland. "Or the Prime Minister."

"The government must not come into this, you know. I

thought that had been made clear. The first contact, the *only* contact so far, was to you. Not us." The Home Secretary was showing signs of alarm. "It must stay that way, it really must. There's been a meeting at Number Ten, you know. Relations with Tripoli have been improving, only a little but it's all a step in the right direction – "

"But Home Secretary, the government's involved automatically by virtue of the fact that it *is* the government. No-one but the government is in a position to order the release of Al Kufra – "

"Which cannot be done under any circumstances, as I've said already."

"Yes." Max was patient. "The fact that it won't be done doesn't alter the basic facts of responsibility. I assure you, however, that 6D2 will do nothing to involve Whitehall *overtly*. Does that help?"

"It puts a different complexion on it," Humphrey Bason admitted. "The press is being held, of course, but it's anyone's guess how long that can be kept up. Especially after that dreadful business in the park last evening." He turned to me. "I understand you were injured, Commander Shaw." He couldn't really miss the bandage.

"Nothing serious, Home Secretary," I said. "Just a graze."

"I believe you've worked with Miss Mandrake in the past?"

"Yes," I said, "and now I'm working *for* her. I aim to get her out from under – don't ask me how, I don't know yet, but I will." Now that I'd been brought into the conversation, I meant to stay in it and put an important point. But first I lifted an eyebrow at Max and he returned it with an almost imperceptible nod. He knew what I was going to say. I went on, "It's always been my experience that these people have to be played along with. In time their approach can soften. Deadlines are extendible just so long as the villains are given a degree of hope."

"Extendible, yes, I agree." Humphrey Bason was feeling his way, largely, I suspected, past the shadow of the Prime Minister. He had come up in the last reshuffle and this was his first hijack – hijack in a sense, anyway, if only of one young

21

woman. "What exactly are you asking?"

I sat forward and fixed him with a hard stare. "I want to be able to release the information, if Whitehall themselves won't do it, that too hard a line is not being taken. That there's room for negotiation."

Bason shook his head. "I doubt if the PM will agree, Commander Shaw, I doubt it very much indeed."

I said, "I'm not suggesting any actual release, Home Secretary. Just a suggestion that it's not being totally cast out."

"A *mendacious* suggestion?"

"You have it precisely."

"Yes, well. Oh, I take your point, indeed. We shall see – I shall be in touch, of course. What you suggest has its merits I dare say. But you know how the PM detests untruths. A very direct and straightforward person."

"And Miss Mandrake?" I asked politely. "Under threat of her life?"

"Oh yes, there is that, I know. Well, perhaps a little duplicity."

I felt relief: we were back to normal political professionalism. Or I hoped so. When Humphrey Bason started to think deeply about it I believed he would respond. Of course, in Worthing West there were plenty of voters who would believe in a firm stand and anyway when the chips were down Al Kufra certainly wasn't going to be released. But if in the interval the Member had done his level best to help a hostage by trying to fool the enemy, there would be any number of old ladies to applaud his humanity, and Worthing West's electoral roll held a very large proportion of old ladies . . .

When Humphrey Bason had gone back to Whitehall, looking uneasy, Max got up and went across to a cupboard which he unlocked. He brought out a whisky decanter and two Caithness crystal glasses. He filled them, adding water – from Perthshire, by courtesy of the Army and Navy Stores, in a tall, cool plastic bottle.

We drank a sardonic health to the Secretary of State for Home Affairs. "A bore," Max said, "and an old woman to boot."

22

"A kindly man," I suggested.

"Let's hope so." Max gave a short laugh. "Forgive me if I make sure."

"How?"

"By ringing the PM and undercutting poor Humphrey, that's how. I can make a very good case and I will." Max lifted his glass and looked through the amber haze towards the sun coming through the big window opposite his desk. "I've often criticised you and Miss Mandrake – your relationship. Right?"

"Right," I said, and waited.

Max said heavily, "I just want her back, that's all. I may be an old bugger, even an old goat . . . but I'm far from dead yet. If you follow."

I grinned tightly. "Jealous?"

"Don't be offensive, Shaw." He turned away from the window and its splendid view over the City of London and points far distant and as he did so one of his telephones burred and he took up the handpiece. He grunted into it, slammed it down again and said, "Your friend Alef Wali. He waits below. Over to you, Shaw."

Alef Wali, I was told before I went into the interrogation room to meet him face to face, had been picked up from his one-room apartment in Stepney by a female 6D2 agent who also came from Egypt. He had been picked up with apparent casualness, actually outside his apartment, in the street, after the agent had made discreet local enquiries as to identity. He had been more than willing to make friends with one of his own countrywomen who had behaved in a very forward fashion, arousing his appetite. He had conceded when she said it would be better at her place, and after something of a walk had got into a taxi with her. Focal House had been a surprise, a very big place for an Egyptian girl to have, and Alef Wali's disembarkation had been assisted by a small revolver from the agent's handbag.

When, a few minutes later, I met him, he complained about this abduction.

I waved a hand. "Purely for your own protection," I said, "since you might not want it known you'd been questioned."

He licked at very full red lips: he was suffering among other things from frustration of his desires – it must have been a shattering disappointment – and he was shaking a little, which could have been fear and probably was. Like Humphrey Bason he was fat; in his case, gross. Physically he resembled quite strongly photographs I'd seen of his one-time monarch, King Farouk, who had also liked women and had looked rather like his own fleshpot. Alef Wali, having less money presumably, was not quite so big but otherwise the description fitted. He asked now, "What is this place, and who are you?"

I temporised. "It's not Scotland Yard anyway, don't worry."

"I'm not bloody worried about no Scotland Yard," he said. I was surprised at his English idiom, but it turned out that he'd been in Britain for some years, in fact since birth, he being a second generation immigrant. In spite of his size he was only twenty-three years of age. "But how about answering the question?"

"No rush," I said evenly. "We're all above board and you're in good hands. It's just that we want to ask *you* some questions, that's all."

"What about?"

"Ibrahim Suwesi, a friend of yours as I understand."

"Oh yes? Who from?"

"A girl," I said. "Now dead. She had a scar and I think she came from Libya. She knew you, you see. And we want to know what *you* know about Ibrahim Suwesi, also dead."

He stared. "I didn't know he was dead!"

"Well, now I'm telling you. I'm also telling you this." I leaned forward towards the Egyptian, the very British Egyptian despite his appearance. "Ibrahim's dead, so is the girl. Two murders – and you were known to both the victims. I'd say you were just a little at risk yourself, Mr Wali. You and maybe a few others. We may be able to help you out of a difficulty. But first, you'll need to give us a few facts."

24

He looked blank. "What sort of facts?"

"Anything you may know about – shall we say, subversive elements with Middle Eastern connections? H'm?"

He shook his head slowly, staring back at me, but there was something in his eye that told me I'd touched a tender spot. He said, "I don't know nothing about that. Subversive elements?"

"Villains," I said. "Men who blow things up, and kidnap people. Terrorists."

"Oh, that."

"Yes. Well?"

Again the shake of the head, and his eyes shifted a little under my hard stare. "No, I don't know nothing. Not my line." He gave a high laugh, a sort of giggle.

"Your line being?"

"Tory rule," he said. "I'm unemployed, droring benefit."

"On which you live?" I stared meaningfully at the full stomach, the fat cheeks.

He said, "Well, there's this and that, like." His eyes narrowed suspiciously. "This the bloody DHSS? You a snooper?"

"No in both cases. It's not that at all. We're not even a government department. You may speak freely, Mr Wali."

"How do I know I can believe you?"

"You don't," I said. "You take us on trust. You're perfectly free to get up and go. But I wouldn't advise that, for reasons aforestated. I think you may be in danger." I didn't really, but it was as good a line as any. "Now – how do you supplement the hand-outs?"

He licked at his lips, then shrugged. After all, it was widely enough known that moonlighters existed. "Window cleaning," he said. "Barman. Chucker-out in a nightclub, Tuesdays." It was Tuesday today. I asked which nightclub.

"Breasty Lil's," he said. "Soho."

I nodded. I knew Breasty Lil's establishment though I'd not seen Alef Wali there; and I knew Breasty Lil, or rather the man who traded under that name, a large fat gay who in fact had, for a man, over-developed breasts that were a help to his transvestism. Breasty Lil, otherwise known as Greasy Todd, had been of help to 6D2 in the past in return for favours granted to keep him out of trouble with the law. I talked a little longer to Alef Wali, drawing him out as far as I reckoned he would go, and I formed the impression that he didn't know much about Ibrahim Suwesi, who had just happened to live in the same neighbourhood. I made no mention, and neither did he, of the Friends of Al Kufra. I let him go, with renewed warnings to watch it and for his own safety not to talk about where he'd spent part of the day.

I didn't tell him that I intended paying a visit to Breasty Lil's. It could be a useful place to stand around in and watch. And listen.

I reported back to Max after Alef Wali had gone. He'd been onto the PM and had found co-operation to the extent that when the Friends of Al Kufra contacted again, which they surely would, the word could be let drop that their requests were being considered at a high level.

"Requests," I said sardonically.

"That's the way it goes, Shaw, and you know it. We're always polite. It helps to fool them." I knew that to be true enough, remembering the hijacked aircraft that had hopped around the Middle East a few years ago, finally coming to rest in Algeria. They'd all been very polite, the authorities addressing the boss gunman as 'Sir' throughout, and providing food and reading matter and doctors in between the casting to the ground of murdered hostages. But the word 'requests' still stuck in my throat like a brick. Anyway, progress, it seemed, had been made. I was about to tell Max about Breasty Lil's when Mrs Dodge, his confidential secretary, came on the line from her office. She had a loud voice and I heard her talking to Max.

"It's the lady, sir, same as before, if you follow me. Shall I put her through?"

"One moment," Max said. He did something with his telephones and gestured me to take up one of the handsets, which I did. "Go ahead, Mrs Dodge."

"Right away, sir."

26

There was a click and a buzz and Mrs Dodge's tones saying "You're through," and then the lady spoke to Max. And to me as well.

"You are the Head of 6D2?"

"Yes. And you, madam?" Max gave me a wink: politeness held.

"You know who I represent. I have news of Miss Mandrake. She is well. But not happy." I felt my fingers tighten, the nails digging into my palms. The frustration was grim. "She wishes to return to you," the voice went on. It was cultured, refined, quite pleasant really, though with a strong accent that I couldn't entirely place but assumed it was Middle Eastern, a fairly wide range and not of much help. "Have you any information to give, please?"

Max said, "I am authorised to say that the matter is being considered."

"Yes?"

"That is all. No further comment."

"I understand. I shall contact you again." There was a pause. I fancied I heard something in the background, a cry and a scuffle, followed by a slap. The voice came in over it again. "I am sorry, just a little trouble. I have to tell you that if matters do not proceed as we wish you will receive in the post a finger of Miss Mandrake."

The call was cut. I got to my feet and lifted both fists in the air. Max said, "Easy, Shaw. It doesn't help. Keep a cool head. Or else," he added with a particular inflexion that I recognised. He would take me off the case at the drop of a hat if I looked like getting frayed at the edges.

I took a grip and said, "Don't worry, I'll behave. If I can't get her out, no-one else can."

"I know. So what's next, Shaw?"

"Breasty Lil's," I said.

3

Tuesday: Alef Wali's night but it couldn't be helped, time was passing. I wouldn't go to Breasty Lil's as myself; I went along to the section where they provide cover and disguise for any situation you care to name. I made my arrangements and said I would be back at 1800 hours to be fitted out. In the long interval I lunched in the agents' dining-room then spent the rest of the time researching the Middle East discs with special reference to Al Kufra, terrorists in general and hijacks. All to no avail; though there was plenty on Al Kufra as I'd read on previous occasions, there was nothing on his Friends, no clues at all. They could of course be a new name for an old group, but then new groups are continually cropping up and this was probably just one more. At 1800 hours sharp I reported back to disguises and after a couple of hours' work by devoted staff, all of whom had at one time been employed in the theatre or television, I emerged as a new man, or anyway a different looking one and in the fashion, the fashion in which I'd visited Breasty Lil's on a number of occasions. Washed-out jeans – Breasty Lil's wasn't a dressy establishment – leather jacket with metal fittings dangling, beads, earrings, dark hair now blond with green and purple streaks and reshaped with starch or something. Small blond moustache and big white boots with thick stockings half-way up my calves.

I left Focal House via the underground parking lot and took the tube to Piccadilly Circus. I walked past the Regent Palace Hotel and into Denman Street where I looked at the cards in the shop windows: strict discipline on offer, French spoken, part-time work wanted, any position, that sort of thing. I had

time to kill for a while yet; I went into a public house loud
with canned music and drank a pint of lager, slowly, keeping
my ears and eyes open as a matter of routine. I thought about
Felicity and I thought about Al Kufra currently in a maximum security prison – Pentonville. He wasn't there for the
Heathrow attempt only: he trailed a long string of terrorist
killings going back over a number of years, some in Britain,
most overseas. Germany, Italy, the Middle East. He'd had
links it was believed with the Baader-Meinhof gang, the IRA,
and a number of Middle Eastern organisations such as the
PLO. Britain was not the only country that had wanted him
behind bars and if we let him go we would not be popular
anywhere much. Felicity was up against the world, and
through her so was I. I wondered how long it would be before
that finger arrived in the mail. Terrorists didn't make empty
threats of that sort and never mind that their deadlines could
be flexible.

In due course I went along to Breasty Lil's, which was
approached from an alley leading off Greek Street, past a row
of dustbins being investigated by stray cats. There was muck
everywhere and I picked my way between fish heads and
rotting vegetables and such. I'd taken out membership a
couple of years earlier, knowing that Greasy Todd had a
number of contacts among the sort of people who could be
useful when you had unanswered questions on your mind. I
also knew that Breasty Lil's was much used by persons with
Middle Eastern connections, which was maybe one contribu-
tory reason for Alef Wali's employment.

I approached the door, the only one in the alley with fresh
paint on it. I rang a bell and waited. When I'd been observed
through the spyhole the door came open and a man, not Alef
Wali, demanded my membership card. This was in the name
of James Gentle.

I was admitted, and climbed the sleazy stairs towards the
sound of music beating down from above. As I walked along a
passage where men and women were entwined I passed a
half-open door. Inside, Greasy Todd was dressing, pulling a
bra over his well-developed breasts. I moved on, skirting

29

round the couples, towards the bar which was at one end of an oblong room in which men and women were dancing, or anyway shuffling around and doing a good deal of feeling meanwhile.

At the bar I asked for lager. Behind the bar I caught a glimpse of Alef Wali in his role of chucker-out, currently downing a drink. I paid eight pounds fifty for the lager and leaned back against the bar. It was not long before I was approached by a girl with very little on. Her breasts jutted; she fitted the name of the establishment.

"Want to dance?" she enquired in a nasal accent, sort of mid-Atlantic.

"All right," I said. We danced, not for very long. That wasn't what she really wanted. Disengaging herself, she suggested a drink. We found a table and the round cost me twenty-nine pounds. The music beat at my eardrums; the room was hot and claustrophobic. She asked if I wanted a good time: there was accommodation for that.

"In the passage?" I asked.

"Upstairs. Seventy."

"Seventy what?"

She giggled. "Pounds."

"Going cheap," I said.

She didn't like it. "That supposed to be funny?"

I shrugged. "Laugh if you want."

"I don't want." I was a bad bet; so was she – we were both wasting our time. She asked, "You gay or what?"

"Yes," I said, and she got up and left. I saw her talking to a man who was swaying his hips in time to the music and patting at his hair-do. She was indicating me and after a while the man swayed over to my table and sat down.

"Hullo, dear," he said. "Lonely?"

"Not very."

"Well, all I can say is you look it. How about buying me a drink?" Red-rimmed eyes leered at me. I made the point that I didn't want to buy him a drink; I had one already, I said. Like the girl, he left me, flouncing away with a hand on one hip. I sat on, just observing. After a short while another girl sat down and stared into my eyes. She was better-looking than the last one and she wasn't after my money.

"Mind if we join you?" she asked.

All the other tables were full; I said I didn't mind. A couple of minutes later the other half of the 'we' turned up, a dark-skinned man, middle-aged, carrying a fortune in two glasses. I had a feeling I'd seen him before but I was unable to place where or when. Someone out of the dodgy past . . . I was intrigued. I didn't appear to register with him and in my disguise there was no reason why I should. I drank my drink and didn't look at the man, didn't show any interest. I listened, of course, but the conversation was innocuous. They discussed forthcoming events. Someone called Mustafa and someone else called Janice would be along soon, the man said, and the girl remarked that she hoped they would be up to form. They both looked as if they were a little high on hard drugs, I thought. And the man's voice, as well as his looks, seemed familiar. But I still couldn't place him.

Mustafa and Janice arrived. The semi-familiar man's hand reached down Janice's back and did something that made her half swoon into his arms. The other girl smiled vaguely, not seeming to mind the opposition. They went away, out through a door beside the bar, and once again I was left alone, though not for long. Two inebriated city gents in business suits sat down without asking if I minded and started guffawing a lot, showing each other photographs.

I was getting nowhere. While this was happening I saw Greasy Todd making an entrance in a long frock and with a startling hair-do, all piled up on his head like a haystack. He swanned around, kissing men and women alike, bestowing the favours of the management but occasionally casting looks of sheer hate at those men who obviously were not of his own persuasion. A drink was poured for him and he leaned back against the bar counter, holding court. As he began scratching at a leg the frock lifted and I saw that his transvestism was not wholly complete: there was a man's sock and a segment of hairy calf.

It wasn't really a good night for my purposes and I felt the pressure of wasting time. When Greasy Todd, his proprietor-ial appearance effected, went back towards his office, I decided to come into the open and ask pertinent questions. I followed behind him and bearded him in his doorway.

"And 'oo are you?" he asked.

"The name's Gentle," I said in a loud voice and in a much lower one against his ear I added, "6D2, Greasy. I'd like a word."

"Oh," he said. "So what's up, then?"

"Nothing to worry you. Just curiosity. May I come in?"

He backed into the office and I followed. I shut the door behind me. He asked, "What's all this, Mr Gentle?"

I grinned. "So you don't recognise me. The name's Shaw."

"Well, I'll be buggered, I'd never 'ave known. What d'you want, eh?"

"Just a little information, Greasy. There's a man I think I've met before, out there." I gestured through the shut door towards the bar. "I'd like to know who he is, that's all."

"Describe 'im, can you?"

I gave a brief description. I added that he was with a girl and had been joined by two friends, Mustafa and Janice, and they'd all gone through the door beside the bar.

Light dawned. "Oh, yes. Like a foursome, they do. Watch-ing each other – you know. I got the paraphernalia upstairs. Whips, bondage, the lot. So what you want to know, Mr Shaw?"

"The identity of the middle-aged one, the dark one."

"Oh yes, you said. Name's Habibi. Behzad Habibi."

"Iranian?"

"I reckon so, yes. Know him, do you?"

I said, "I don't know for sure. Not under that name, any-way. Do you know anything about him, Greasy? What he does, that sort of thing? Address, perhaps?"

Primly Greasy Todd said, "I'm not at liberty to disclose information about members, Mr Shaw, you know that, or ought."

I shrugged. "Past favours, Greasy."

"Yes, but still . . ."

"Favours don't have to continue, Greasy, do they? You don't want Breasty Lil's to come under close surveillance, do you? From the Yard?"

He sniffed. "Them sods are always around anyway."

"But not too close for comfort. They could get a lot closer and you know it, Greasy."

"Threats now, is it?"

"Yes," I said. "With regret. But what I'm after is important. Vital. I'll go the whole way to get what I want."

Greasy Todd didn't like it at all. He turned away from me and sat down at his desk. The office was more like a star's dressing-room, with a long mirror for Greasy to look at himself in, clothes everywhere, both male and female, and there was a shelf of make-up, lipstick, eye shadow, powder, things for plucking eyebrows, deodorant, setting lotion. There was a strong smell of scent. Greasy Todd sat for a while looking disturbed and then said, "No comebacks, then. I don't get involved. I don't get named. I 'ave me business to think of, right?"

"Right," I said.

He nodded and told me that so far as he knew Behzad Habibi was an agent.

"Agent," I repeated in a flat tone. "So what's that supposed to cover?"

"None of my business to know that."

"Make a few guesses, then. It won't be held against you."

Reluctantly he said, "Call girls. Makes a bomb. Which is more than I do."

"All right," I said, "I'm not an income tax inspector. Address, Greasy?"

He sighed and ferreted about in a drawer of the desk, bringing out a large book. He scanned this, riffling the pages through, then said, "'E gives a club address. Search me if 'e lives there or not. Lion and Palm Tree, Curzon Street." He closed the book and pushed it back in the drawer. "That's all I know."

*

33

The fighting started before I'd left Breasty Lil's. I'd just come out of Greasy Todd's office boudoir when one of the city gents who'd come to my table fell over a fornicating couple when he was on his way to the lavatory. He started a semi-drunken argument and the girl who'd been tripped over hit him on the head with the spiked heel of her shoe, very hard so that the steel tip penetrated. There was a lot of blood and people started screaming, the hurt man's friend pounded up from behind, and behind him came Alef Wali, butting through with his stomach and fists. In no time the thing became general, bottles and glasses were brought into play, as were the tables. The bar itself became a shambles of broken glass and spilt expensive liquor. Greasy Todd stood in his doorway, yelling.

No-one took any notice. The exit route was well and truly blocked with bodies piled on top of one another. I saw Alef Wali pick one up and throw it down the narrow staircase, which fell steeply to the passage below. A man came at me with the jagged end of a broken bottle, and cut my arm before I sent him down with a heavy blow to the jaw. A woman, his companion I think, rushed from behind with what looked like a hat pin, very sharp. It was aimed for my eyes. Unchivalrously I kneed her in the groin and she clapped a hand to the region and went down with a shriek of pain that made me think she was no woman after all. I knew it was no use expecting Greasy Todd to use his telephone to call the fuzz. He would be hoping the fuzz would be far away until Alef Wali and his mates – I identified three other men who seemed to be fellow chuckers-out – had gained control and emptied the customers out into the alley.

Then something else happened: an ashtray with some burning butts in it got scattered onto a small pile of paper napkins that had been ejected from the bar counter in the fracas. Flames curled up and there was a strong smell of smoke and a lot more shrieking and yelling and all present dissolved their differences in needless panic and went in a rush for the stairs, where they stuck.

I shrugged and put the fire out, using an unbroken soda siphon. But the word, and the smoke, had spread upstairs, and down them, in a tizzy, came Janice and Mustafa with Behzad Habibi and his own woman, all of them semi-clad.

I said, "No rush, ladies and gentlemen. If I were you, I'd wait till the gangway's clear."

"Where's the fire?" Behzad Habibi asked.

"Out," I said.

"You sure?"

"I put it out myself," I said modestly. "No trouble."

"Ha. Good." Behzad Habibi turned round to reassure the others and I saw his back: he was wearing only his underpants. That was when memory returned in a rush. Even the name I'd known him by, once: Safi Suduteh. On his back, just above the waistline, was a tattoo. It was of a big, leggy spider, hairy, purple in colour with faded blue spots. And it identified Behzad Habibi in a flash. If I hadn't already known I was up against extreme danger, I would have known for sure now. And something personal as well, which made it the more dangerous. Behzad Habibi turned round again and I saw that he still hadn't recognised me. Which was just as well. I could have become just another casualty in a nightclub brawl, and not the only death at that. The word spread back from the mob jamming the staircase that the man who'd taken the steel heel was as dead as mutton. Also that Alef Wali, with a knife blade deep in his back, had joined in the after-life.

Soon after that the fuzz arrived in strength. The fighting had spilled over into the alley and beyond, into Greek Street.

I was arrested along with all those who hadn't managed to get clear before the fuzz came. I was manhandled along to a Black Maria together with my immediate companions – Mustafa, Janice, Safi Suduteh alias Behzad Habibi and the second woman, plus some others. We were taken to a police station and after a long wait I was taken under escort to an interrogation room where two plain-clothes men started the questioning. Each of the battling customers was being questioned separately; this was now the start of a murder investigation.

I was asked my name. I gave it – the right one.

"Todd says James Gentle."

35

"Cover," I said. "And my real name's not to be mentioned where the mob might hear it."

A fist smacked into a palm. "Who's giving the orders around here?"

"I am," I said. "And you're going to take due note unless you want Whitehall on your backs." That was when I mentioned 6D2 and asked to be put in immediate touch with Focal House. The two dicks conferred together in a corner of the room; they were not taking any chances, it seemed. They agreed to contact Focal House and once they had the attitude changed. But still no chances; I was taken, head under someone's jacket at my own request, out to a police car and was driven to Focal House. They took me inside, head still covered, and the duty officer was sent for to the checkpoint. I was identified, though one of our disguise experts had first to be brought along to affirm my story and my appearance. Then the fuzz left, uttering a formal warning that charges might yet be brought, but I wasn't worried at all about that. 6D2 was cast iron and Max had plenty of strings to pull if anyone became officious.

I was much more worried about Behzad Habibi, even though he was currently in police custody. I was so worried that I persuaded the duty officer to call Max. Max, I said, would want to be there. If he wasn't informed pronto, someone's head would roll. I went along to the staff quarters while I waited for Max and cleaned away the disguise and got back into my normal clothing. While I did so I thought about the past, and about Safi Suduteh, or Behzad Habibi, from Iran.

It had been three years earlier, on a small island in the Persian Gulf. I had been with Felicity on a job involving both Iran and Saudi Arabia. We were working, vicariously, for the Saudis, an intricate investigation broadly concerned, naturally enough, with British oil interests. Felicity herself had been the one who had cornered Safi Suduteh, whose mission for Teheran had been, in fact, to liquidate the two of us. When Felicity had brought him to the island at gunpoint aboard a small power-boat to make the rendezvous with me, we'd had some Saudis with us. The Saudis were just as bloodthirsty as the Iranians and they had wanted to kill Suduteh there and then. He had been responsible, as a member of an organisation known as the Spiders of Mount Hira, for the murders of a large number of Saudis, plus three big scale acts of terrorism in their country.

But the Saudis were in radio communication with Riyadh and when they reported the capture of Safi Suduteh they were given unequivocal orders that he was not to be killed. He would be more valuable alive. So Suduteh had lived; but the Saudis wanted their personal pound of flesh and they had tortured him to the point of a gibbering and abject plea for mercy, with Felicity forced to look upon his shame – not nice, for an Iranian to whom women were very second-class citizens, best hidden behind the veil. When the torture had stopped, and after Suduteh had recovered a little, he swore an oath that one day he would have the woman in his grasp and he would torture her as he had been tortured, and he would kill her.

I had seen the purple spider tattooed on his back, the mark of allegiance of the Spiders of Mount Hira. Now, having seen it again and recognised it, I knew why I hadn't recognised the whole man more quickly. For one thing he had worn a heavy beard then; now it was gone. For another, the Saudis had cut off his nose during the torture. Now he had another nose, a beautifully done graft or whatever, no signs of the plastic surgery showing. Also, I hadn't known that he was not still in custody in Riyadh. He was in fact the last person I would have expected to find in Breasty Lil's that night.

"So what now?" Max asked. "The connection with Miss Mandrake's kidnap is pretty tenuous, isn't it?"

"A hunch," I said. "That threat. It wasn't lightly made. Far from it." My thoughts went backwards. "I can hear him now, Max. The venom."

Max nodded. "But we need something stronger as a link with the Friends of Al Kufra – "

"That," I said, "I aim to find. If it exists."

"Do you want him brought here, Shaw?" Just as soon as I'd reported, Max had dug the Metropolitan Police Commissioner out of bed by telephone: the man now known as Behzad Habibi would be held in the nick pending further enquiries. But I didn't believe we'd get much out of him by questioning and I said so.

"I'd rather follow my own line," I said. "See where he leads. Do we know anything about the Lion and Palm Tree, Curzon Street?"

Max shrugged. "It's known. Watched from time to time. Nothing much, though."

"Residential?"

"Not exactly! Short periods only, very handy for some."

"Then he's not likely to be living there," I said. Then I added, "The mere fact that he's turned up at this particular moment . . . have we ever been informed of a release, Max?"

"We have not," he said. "Release or escape – I don't know. Either it's very recent or the Saudis have a reason for not revealing it."

"Loss of face, if it's an escape?"

"Could be, I suppose. I'll be contacting our man in Riyadh – should have had his nose a damn sight closer to the ground. But you were saying?"

"Just that his turning up now, in London, could be somewhat pointed."

"Towards Miss Mandrake and the Friends of Al Kufra?"

"Yes," I said. "But I still don't believe questioning would help. I'd like him lulled. Then I'll be finding out."

"You hope. Make it fast. Remember the deadline," Max said, as though I needed any reminder. "Do I take it you're asking for him to be released from custody?"

"That's what I'm asking," I said. "If it helps to satisfy the police, I can confirm that Suduteh – Behzad Habibi – had nothing to do with the deaths in Breasty Lil's."

Max nodded. "And the Saudis?"

"Bugger the Saudis, Max. Riyadh hasn't kept us informed. Officially we don't know who the man is, beyond the fact he was someone involved in a brawl."

"All right," Max said. "I'll go along with you." He added a warning. "Don't lose him." Then he put through another call to the Yard. I was dropped by a 6D2 car at the nick where Behzad Habibi was being held. I had words with the chief superintendent in charge. He'd already had his orders from on high but he didn't like it. I asked him if Behzad Habibi had said anything in the meantime, and he hadn't. All he'd said was that his name was Behzad Habibi, his address was the Lion and Palm Tree, Curzon Street, and he wanted the club informed so that his car could be brought round.

"Some people," he said witheringly. "What do they think we are, bloody messenger boys?"

I said. "I'd like him pandered to – if you don't mind. I'd like his car brought. But not just yet."

I had the Focal House car take me back to my flat to pick up my own car and then went back fast to report at the nick. Then I got into my car and waited. I had a strong hunch that Behzad Habibi didn't intend just going back to the Lion and Palm Tree. He was going to shift berth – why, I couldn't guess, unless he thought circumstances had forced him a little too far into the open and he'd decided to do some covering up. By rights he should now be happy: he was to be released with assurances that he was in the clear as regards what had happened in Breasty Lil's. Within the next fifteen minutes a big Saab pulled up outside the nick and a flabby-looking man got out, went inside and after a short delay came out with Safi Suduteh alias Behzad Habibi and the Saab went off fast with me behind, heading not towards Curzon Street but making for Bond Street and Marble Arch and Edgware.

At what had once been Staples Corner the Saab, two cars ahead of me, turned onto the M1 and began taking it really fast. After we'd passed the Scratchwood service area I let a couple more cars come between us and then settled down for the chase.

There was a certain amount of heavy stuff on the move through the early hours but on the whole the traffic was light and the Saab made very good speed, with me varying my distance. From time to time I overtook, mostly just after a feed-in, and then I would allow myself to be overtaken in my turn and dropped back behind artics and so on, taking myself out of the Saab's rearview mirror. We stayed on the M1 right through to the interchange onto the M62, from which we took the M606 into Bradford.

By the time we got into Bradford there was a lot more traffic on the move: it was daylight now. Following the Saab at a discreet distance through the outskirts I found a good deal of dereliction, old, deserted, blank-faced warehouses of an earlier generation, and there were road works, diversions and contra-flows in places. As we neared the city centre, the Saab jumped a set of lights. I was held up by the two cars in front of me, and I lost Behzad Habibi. Furiously, impotently, I cursed and drove on, trapped in the stream of traffic. No sign of the Saab; somewhere in the city centre I followed signs to a car park, which I found on a cleared piece of ground, quite handy. Sick with myself, I left the car and went on foot to find police HQ. I'd not been in Bradford before and I found it very different from what I'd expected from reading Priestley and others: the place had been refurbished, modernised, almost rebuilt. So many new buildings that sat uneasily with the old of which there were not many – some old bank buildings and insurance companies, the rest brashly modern. There were a lot of Pakistanis around to lend the old city a new colour. At police HQ I identified myself and asked for a line to Focal House in London. Max was still there; after I'd left him he'd turned into the bedroom in his office suite rather than go home. He said he'd just got up and had been brought the day's news-papers. He said that rather ominously, but waited for my confession before unburdening his own mind.

He said, "Too bad, Shaw. But these things happen. I rely on you to pick him up again. He may come to the surface. Have you read the papers?"

"No chance yet," I said. "I – "

"Get them. It's broken. And God damn the gutter press. Keep in touch, Shaw." Then he cut the call, leaving me somewhat in the air. I found some newspapers in the nick, and read them whilst breakfasting in the canteen. One at least of the headlines was lurid. UNDERCOVER GIRL FALLS FOUL OF SEX MONSTER. So far as I knew, the Friends of Al Kufra, or anyway the Spiders of Mount Hira, were not sex-orientated though they might be monsters; but of course sex has always to be dragged in somehow to make it all the more interesting. God alone knew where the press had got it all from, but in basis, leaving out the sex angle, they'd got it more or less right. Felicity Mandrake had been kidnapped and was being held hostage against the release of the killer Al Kufra in Pentonville. A number of opinions had been canvassed. Government sources would say nothing, not even to confirm or deny the facts. Some trendy lefties had expressed the view that Al Kufra should be handed over without delay. A minor official in the Foreign Office had said that if the reports were true, as to which he was not in a position to comment, then the Prime Minister would make the right decision. There were profiles of various Middle Eastern leaders, and a catalogue of Al Kufra's crimes including a rehash of the Heathrow outrage that had been nipped in the bud just in time. Even 6D2 was referred to by name, which I knew would have maddened Max.

As for me, it was impasse.

But late that night after a frustrating day a very curious sequence of events took place.

4

Behzad Habibi might or might not still be in Bradford but I could only make the assumption that he was. I had decided not to return to London; I wanted to be on the spot. It was possible, even likely I thought, that Felicity was up here in Bradford – that was, still making the basic diagnosis that Behzad Habibi was in cahoots with the Friends of Al Kufra, perhaps just for those personal reasons in regard to Felicity. When an Iranian swears an oath of vengeance, he uses every endeavour to keep it. All that could turn out to be way off the beam but it was all I had to work on so I stuck with it.

I conferred with Bradford CID. There were, as I knew, any number of immigrants in the city but these were mostly Indians and Pakistanis. Not many known Iranians or Saudis or others from contiguous Middle Eastern countries. The CID would be keeping their eyes and ears open. I pondered the possibilities of making myself into a magnet to attract Behzad Habibi, who would be keen enough to get his hands on me once he knew I was around. I could become conspicuous by asking questions in certain quarters as indicated by the CID: they knew just where I could land myself in trouble. Once I'd flushed Behzad Habibi it would be up to me to turn the tables fast. But I still didn't see that as the best way. I was dead sure he wouldn't talk. I had to get deep, find the mainspring behind Behzad Habibi. Blunt methods were out.

About lunchtime news came through from Whitehall, via Focal House: Al Kufra was being moved from Pentonville under a very strong police guard, with armoured vehicles provided by the army, police patrol cars, outriders, and a helicopter hovering throughout. The police would be armed. Al Kufra, in order to throw off the Friends, was not being moved to another civil prison. He was being taken to Stirling Castle in Scotland, where he would be incarcerated in a secure dungeon beneath the regimental HQ of the Argyll and Sutherland Highlanders who, although their depot was at Glencorse Barracks in Edinburgh with the rest of the Scottish Division, still maintained a presence in Stirling.

On the security line I asked Max, "Does this mean an attack's thought likely, a cutting-out operation?"

"Yes. If Miss Mandrake's not enough – "

"Have they contacted again?"

"No. I'll let you know the moment they do. There's been nothing at all." This, I guessed, was a reference to the threat of the finger in the post. This was a big relief but it could be only temporary. After lunch, taken like breakfast in the canteen, I booked myself into the Norfolk Gardens Hotel for some much-needed sleep. I intended to do some anonymous prowling during the night in areas of the city that according to CID might be propitious. Tired though I was, sleep didn't come quickly. I was too conscious of what was implicit in the move of Al Kufra to maximum-plus security in an unlikely place of incarceration: Al Kufra was not going to be handed over whatever became of Felicity. I never thought he would be, but this was the ultimate confirmation. The end of hope, really. I hadn't made much of a showing so far and the hours were ticking away towards that deadline.

Evening came, and night.

I drove round the city, establishing my geography of a place not previously known to me. Not my own car: an unmarked police car, with driver, had been put at my disposal, and the officer knew his way around, knew the places I would want to see. There were night spots, not unlike Breasty Lil's as I described it to my driver.

It was just after 2 a.m. when the call came through from police HQ. There had been a report from North Yorkshire police and I was wanted back at the nick. My driver got me back in record time and I was given the facts, such as they were known, by the duty inspector. North Yorkshire police had found something strange going south from the Dales – from Swaledale, near the tiny village of Muker. An undertaker's hearse, with coffin. The hearse bore a Bradford registration. It had been stopped in Hawes in Wensleydale by the patrol car that had followed it down from Muker. The name of a Bradford undertaker had been given, and the driver of the hearse had told his story. The body in the coffin was that of a farmer who had died the previous day and, having been Bradford-born eighty-four years earlier, had expressed a wish to be buried there.

"Weird wish," the duty inspector commented. "Me, I'd sooner be left in Swaledale if I'd spent my life there. However, here's the nub, Commander: the hearse driver and his two mates were from the Middle East. Which is why you were wanted back here . . . to us currently, the Middle East means you."

"Right," I said. "Anything else?"

"Yes. The circumstances being at that hour of the night suspicious, the North Yorkshire blokes took a close look at the coffin. They ordered the lid to be removed – their duty, as they saw it, but also their personal mistake. The occupants of the hearse opened fire . . . silenced revolvers. One of the car's crew had his head blown off, the other got a graze that concussed him. When he came round the hearse had vanished. He then reported in on his radio." The duty inspector rubbed a hand across his moustache. "Well, sir? What do you make of all that, eh?"

I was stumped and said so. The contents of the coffin would have been of interest undoubtedly. Was there a body, or was there something else? The inspector said all undertakers in Bradford would be contacted as fast as possible, but I had a feeling it wouldn't be fast enough. I racked my brains for ideas . . . guns, aboard a hearse. A coffin, contents unknown. Middle Eastern persons involved, and Behzad Habibi in the Bradford area. A Bradford undertaker . . . the name of whom as reported by North Yorkshire police was not known to the duty inspector, who had consulted a list of such.

44

Behzad Habibi, and guns. Behzad Habibi was used to guns and explosives. He'd done plenty of blow-ups under his real name of Safi Suduteh.

Explosives in a coffin?

Something clicked. I said, "That road convoy, Inspector. Al Kufra, en route for Stirling. What's the nearest it's going to be to North Yorkshire . . . on the M6, presumably, somewhere west of – "

"No, sir. It's been diverted. It would have come off the M1 at Junction 19 but the southern end of the M6 is blocked across all six carriageways by a big pile-up . . . an artic crossed the central reservation. The new route's M18 and A1 to Scotch Corner, then A66 to M6 at Penrith." The inspector picked up a sheet of paper. "It'll be in the area till around 0730 hours."

I checked my watch. "Two and a half hours. Where will it be at, say, 0630?"

"Probably around ten miles south of Boroughbridge," he said.

"Not the motorway section. And a longish way in North Yorkshire. Plenty of likely spots for an ambush. I wonder!"

"Ambush by hearse, sir?"

"You wouldn't suspect a hearse, would you? A hearse with a loaded coffin. Waiting in a side road. Explosives. Grenades, say, to halt the head of the column . . . after a rendezvous with a back-up party to shoot down the escort – something like that?"

"Could be, sir." The inspector sounded doubtful, as though I was fantasising too far. "Wouldn't work now, anyway. A hearse is going to stand out a mile, after this."

"There'll be plenty of hearses around, genuine funerals."

"Not on the main arterial routes," he said.

"No. I take your point, Inspector. That patrol maybe nipped something in the bud."

I was convinced there was a link. The Friends of Al Kufra were not pinning too many hopes on their hostage. Foiled perhaps this time, they might dream up something else before

45

that road convoy reached Stirling Castle – they had a few hours in which to react and regroup as it were. Of course, it might not be long enough, in which case it would perforce be back to Felicity Mandrake. In the meantime I could only await the results of the police check on the funeral establishments and I didn't expect much from them. It was just a routine that had to be gone through. None of the respectable businesses would be involved; though admittedly nefarious persons could be making unauthorised use of their vehicles and equipment, and this was the line the nick would be pursuing.

As it happened, something did turn up.

The police made a discovery: a back-street funeral director's sleazy establishment where obsequies were done on the cheap, mostly but not wholly for the immigrant population. This establishment was not on the list of such. The p.c. had gone in for a check. There was a good deal of shiftiness around and no hearse, though there were a number of coffins. The hearse, the proprietor told the police, was out on a job. The name of the deceased was, nicely anonymous, Patel. The investigating officer was not entirely satisfied. He'd gone back to his patrol car and called the nick, and I was informed.

I went along.

I asked about the hearse.

"Not back yet, sir," the constable said.

"Have you gone through the place?" I asked. He hadn't; he'd decided, having reported in, to wait for me and the hearse. I said we wouldn't go on waiting for the hearse to show. It began to look as though the police had found the right place, though when the constable had enquired the registration number of the hearse it had not been the number of the one stopped in Hawes. But that didn't prove anything in my view; persons with things to hide don't always speak the truth. If we'd struck gold, that hearse would by now be anywhere but Bradford.

I told the proprietor I wanted all the coffins opened up. He was very co-operative, suspiciously so. None of the coffins were screwed down, no corpses in transit, so the lids were just lifted off, one by one – there were eleven of them, all very basic. I asked for a tape measure and I checked for false bottoms: I found nothing. It looked like stalemate; but the premises could be put under surveillance for what that might be worth. I doubted the worth: I believed the hearse wouldn't come back and if we'd found the right place, neither would Behzad Habibi be likely to show.

I told the proprietor I wanted to look around the rest of the premises and his manner changed. There was, he said, nothing to see, no more coffins, just the yard, the garage for the hearse, and the coffin-maker's shop in the rear.

"Just the same," I said, "I'd like to look." I gestured to the constable to accompany me and we went out into the yard. The garage stood empty, the doors open. There wasn't much in the yard, just the clutter of any yard: dustbins, a scatter of wood shavings from the coffin-maker's shop, a length of hose for washing down the hearse, a tabby cat cleaning itself in a corner. But while I took my look at what was to be seen, I heard sounds from the coffin-maker's shop, a kind of dragging. Still accompanied by the constable, I went towards it, fast, and as I did so I glanced at the proprietor and saw the look of tension, of fear.

I shoved a door open and went in. I saw three men who could have been Iranians. They were carrying a coffin and it seemed to be heavy. Arms, explosives? As I entered they put the coffin down and their expressions made me go for my shoulder holster. I heard the constable's warning shout and a scuffle behind me. Then I heard the muffled sound of a silenced revolver and a moment later something heavy took me on the side of my head.

I came round in blinding pain accompanied by a feeling of nausea. I hadn't been out for long, I gathered: the body of the constable was still there on the floor of the coffin-shop and blood was being self-mopped by the piles of wood shavings. The coffin was on the floor and four armed men were looking down at me. My lips felt very dry; I licked at them. My eyes hurt and I closed them against an overhead light. I heard a

47

low conversation, not in English. Opening my eyes again, I saw two of the men unscrewing the lid of the coffin they'd been carrying. When the lid came off I was grabbed and hoisted to my feet and I saw that there was a shrouded body in the coffin. I didn't get much of a look; when I was up, a fist crashed against my jaw, three times, and I went out again.

That time I must have been unconscious for a very long while. I had no idea at all of what had gone on in the meantime when finally I did come round. It was a while before I could orientate myself. I was lying on something hard and there was a lot of vibration and a swinging motion that did nothing for my renewed nausea. There was a draught blowing around me and I was in darkness. After a while I realised I was in a moving vehicle, probably in the back of a lorry or van being driven fast. My hands were tied behind my back; my ankles were tied as well and there was a gag in my mouth. I sweated with pain and nausea, felt I might choke if the gag wasn't removed soon. After a little more time I began to see my surroundings: the darkness was not total. The rear doors were not a close fit, hence the draught, and some light came through, plus a little more from a dirty window giving onto the cab.

Alongside me, I saw a man sitting in, of all things, an easy chair. He looked Oriental. He had a gun aimed at me. On my other side I saw the coffin. When the van took a bend, the coffin slid against me and the easy chair slid a little also. I hoped the man's finger wasn't too closely hooked around the trigger of his revolver. When he saw that I was more or less compos mentis he spoke to me in English of a sort.

He said, grinning, "You feel bad."

I couldn't answer through the gag. The man spoke again. "Do not make attempts."

As if I could.

He became informative. "It will be not long now, Commander Shaw."

The use of my name came as no surprise. I'd dropped into the right place and maybe Behzad Habibi had been called in to identify me – he would recognise me easily enough out of

48

the disguise as used in Breasty Lil's. What I did wonder through the pain and my generally poor condition was what the man meant by 'not long now'. Not long till we got somewhere, or not long for me to live?

He became more informative and still grinned, still kept the revolver nicely aimed. "In the coffin is Miss Mandrake," he said.

That piece of information numbed me. I don't think I really took it in right away. I found myself wondering if she'd been in the coffin all the way down through the Dales from up by Muker, through to Hawes where the first policeman had been gunned down. Felicity, not the hypothetical arms or explosives. That would knock the theory of an ambush of the road convoy – which could now be well north, even arrived at Stirling; I had no idea of the time. And I could ask no questions. I became inertly frantic, thinking about Felicity and what horrors she might have undergone. Thinking about how she'd been let down by 6D2. How she'd been let down by me, though Max wouldn't have agreed with that. He'd have said we'd done all we could. Miracles could not be expected. That was no doubt true but it didn't help now. I was in the throes of self-recrimination. Not just me, of course: Whitehall should have played much more along the lines I'd suggested at the start. It hadn't been enough just to let it be known to the Friends of Al Kufra that their demands were being considered. They should have been more forthcoming in an attempt to save a hostage, a helpless girl. Now, of course, once the move of Al Kufra to Stirling had become known, as certainly it would, there would have come an automatic end to belief in the British government's veracity.

Hence Felicity in the coffin? I wondered what they meant to do next.

There was no further information; the man had dried up. The drive continued, a very long way though I still had no idea of how much time was passing. My tied body was racked with the bumps and vibrations, the swing round bends and sharp corners, the latter becoming more and more frequent as the day wore on. It seemed a never-ending journey and I had the idea it was growing colder, though that could have been due to my inert state, the inaction.

When we did stop, it was after a reduction to very slow speed over very rough ground. Quite a long way. When finally we came to a halt there was a delay and then the rear doors were opened up and I was lifted and carried out and dumped on the ground, muddy ground. It was fully dark so I saw little, but felt a keen wind and smelled a farmyard smell, and then saw a light in a window of a building. I was lifted again soon after and carried into the building, what looked like a farm kitchen, old-fashioned and primitive. There was a plain scrubbed table, a long stone sink, a dresser, a Calor gas cooker as well as a kitchen range that appeared to be no longer in use – the kitchen was very cold – a store cupboard and a recess in a thick stone wall that could once have been used for baking bread. The walls were whitewashed. We were in no town; my guess was somewhere well north, and deep in remote country-side. Possibly Cumbria or Northumberland. Or even farther north.

There was a basket-work chair. I was told to sit in it. With difficulty I did so. One of the men – one of the Iranians from Bradford – held a gun on me. Then the coffin was brought in from the van and put on the table in the middle of the kitchen.

5

They took the lid off. Then they pulled away part of the shroud.

I saw Felicity. The men were watching me. One of them, the Oriental who'd been with me in the back of the van, was grinning. I tried to think calmly, found there was nothing to think about except what had happened to Felicity, and why. You don't normally kill hostages – not so early in the proceedings, certainly not when you have only the one, and I was a very recent acquisition myself. Then another of the men came forward and bent over Felicity's head and held a small mirror to her lips.

He showed it to me. "See," he said. "There is breathing. So."

I stared. Relief swept over me. I said nothing, waiting for the man to speak again.

He did. "Use of drugs, Commander Shaw. Numbing ones. Soon she will recover. Can always be drugged again. No harm ensues."

I looked again at the coffin. For the first time I saw, in the side by Felicity's head, a round hole in the wood. A hole for air. The man who had spoken – he told me later that he was a North Korean – saw where I was looking and from a pocket brought out a plug, the circle of wood that had been removed to make the air-hole. He inserted it and you would scarcely have noticed anything had been cut through; it was a perfect job. There was, he said, another on the other side of the coffin.

I saw movement then. Felicity was beginning to stir and soon I was able to hear her breathing. Her head turned and lifted a little and she saw me. She didn't speak but I saw the tears spilling from her eyes to run down deathly white cheeks. The men lifted her from the coffin and carried her out of the room and I heard her crying as she went. It wasn't like Felicity. I wondered if they had broken her spirit. Hopefully it was just the effects of the drug.

Still sitting in the chair, still tied, still with the guns handy, I was questioned by the party spokesman.

"What is being done with Al Kufra, Commander Shaw?"

"I don't know," I said. "I've been out of touch for a while."

"Come now. You are close to the men of power. Please answer."

I said more or less what I'd said before. "You know as much as me."

"We know that he has been moved to Stirling Castle."

"And you didn't get him before arrival."

"Not important. He will be got out but we do not wish bloodshed. Please tell us what your government intends to do, Commander Shaw."

I said, "You'll have been told your demands are being considered. That's all I know. I'm not privy to Whitehall's thoughts."

This was considered. "Perhaps not. You will have theories. Tell, please."

"You'll just have to wait," I said. "Governments move slowly. And I haven't any theories. It's not my job to theorise. I just obey orders. That's all."

"Your orders were to extract Miss Mandrake?"

There was no point in denying the obvious. "Yes," I said.

"There are other orders. Tell, please."

"No other orders." This happened to be the truth. I'd had no orders from Max, as such. I knew what was expected of me and there had been no need of detailed instructions. In the game of undercover agents, you act as the situation dictates, responding to events when you can't control them.

"I do not believe," the Oriental said calmly and patiently. "You have been sent to frustrate the hand-over of Al Kufra.

52

Your government is mendacious, speaking with forked tongue. They seek to deceive by easy words of considering our demands." He paused. "Not so, Commander Shaw?"

"Have it your own way," I said, "since you won't believe me anyway." I couldn't see the point of the interrogation, really. Hijackers, kidnappers, always know very well that there can never be a compromise. Either the aircraft, the train, the ship or whatever, gets blown up as per threat or it does not. Similarly, in such a situation as this one, the man in demand is released or he is not. All that's really at stake is the fate of the villains; that can be the only compromise – safe conduct for them. And, of course, I knew that no-one in government was going to release Al Kufra. Far too much was at stake internationally. Thinking along international lines, before any more questions could be asked of me, I said I had one of my own to ask. How was it that persons from the Orient were involved in what was purely a Middle Eastern affair?

The little man seemed put out by that. "You do not know, Commander Shaw?"

I said I had no idea. Then he said that was the point of the questioning; I was fogged by that. But that was when he told me that he and certain others were North Korean nationals and he wanted to know how much the British government knew about a North Korean connection. I genuinely didn't know; but thereafter they did their best to extract the information that I didn't have.

Torture had never been a purely eastern nastiness. We in England had had our oubliettes in the Middle Ages, our racks and Iron Maidens, foot presses and thumb-screws and pincers, while in Scotland they had favoured the pinniewinks, the caspitaws and the tosots. But these men were good at it and they were refined, up to a point. They used the water treatment, during which you get the sensation of drowning. The farmhouse had been modernised to the extent of having had electricity installed and the men made use of that too. I was brought pretty low one way and another, but it didn't do them any good. I had no knowledge to impart in any case. But they

53

were determined to make quite sure, so they used Felicity. She was brought back to the kitchen, on her feet by this time and being supported by two of the Bradford Iranians. She was sat on a hard upright chair close to the table.

The North Korean spoke to me. He said, "Warning was passed about the finger."

"You bastard," I said. He just grinned as usual. From the drawer in the dresser, after some foraging about, he extracted a carving knife, very thin from constant use over many years of farmhouse beef. Felicity was held fast, and her left hand was clamped down to the table by one of the Iranians, and the North Korean approached with the knife, the blade of which he laid on the top joint of her little finger.

"So," he said, looking across at me. "You tell, please?"

Having nothing to say, I said nothing. I was still tied up and helpless. The blade pressed down. Felicity caught her breath. I saw the run of blood.

"You tell, please?"

I said, "I have genuinely nothing to tell. That's the truth. So help me God." I felt sweat pouring down my face, never mind the kitchen's dank coldness. I was sweating all over as Felicity gave a low cry. I yelled obscenities at the men; 'bastards' was the least of it. Then there came a diversion, obviously very unexpected by any of the men who were no doubt unused to life in what I was now convinced was northern England, somewhere well up in the fells and probably not far from the Scottish border. There was a devastating roar overhead, very close, very low, as if the farmhouse was about to be attacked. I recognised the roar and thunder of the Tornadoes of the RAF, on normal low-flying exercises. I'd suffered from them myself once or twice when in the north, the tremendous speed, the devastatingly sudden appearance of an aircraft right overhead, often dangerous to one's driving on the narrow roads through the northern fell country. But I'd not known them to operate at night before.

Anyway, they caused consternation. The Iranians ran about in circles like scared rabbits and they left Felicity alone. There were two more overhead sorties and then the racket went away. I made the most of it. I said the RAF had probably been alerted and any minute the fuzz would be on its way in. Someone, I said, could have tailed the van and now they were stuck with the result. The Iranians jabbered a lot in their own language and they shelved the removal of Felicity's finger. The coffin was carried away somewhere with Felicity back in it after the North Korean had used a hypodermic. I was taken out into the farmyard, still tied and now once again gagged and with a bag tied over my head for good measure. I felt myself lifted, with much stertorous breathing and heaving, then a rope was put around me and hauled taut beneath my armpits and I was lowered with a cranking sound for a long way before coming to rest on something lumpy and smelly. I was, it seemed, in a dried-out well. I tried not to think about what I guessed was beneath me. I spent the rest of the night alternating between troubled sleep and a wonderment about that North Korean involvement. When morning came the men returned and hoisted me out from what I saw, when they removed the bag from my head, was indeed a well. Looking down, I confirmed what I had passed the night with, or anyway on top of: two bodies, an old man and an old woman, presumably the late farmer and his wife, slaughtered in the interest of temporary housing for the Friends of Al Kufra.

The men were in a nasty mood. "You speak lies," the North Korean said. "There was no RAF. No policemen. No danger to us."

I shrugged. At least the villains had been given a night's anxiety. I supposed that if any police really had turned up and had shown an interest in the well, they would simply have been gunned down and then there would have been an exodus. It was so simple, just to gun people down. However, I believed that I'd learned something that could be worth bearing in mind: when the panic had started they would surely have moved out before the arrival of the fuzz – if they'd had somewhere else to go to.

It turned out that I was wrong on that. Maybe they just hadn't wanted to get on the road and meet the fuzz coming in on the way out. Maybe they'd relied wholly on gun power, the immediate shoot-up of a patrol car and its radio, after which they could have pushed on untailed.

We did move out after the coffin, no longer required for some reason or other, had been dropped down the well on top of the bodies, and after a scratch breakfast had been provided for all hands: bread and margarine, and water from the tap in the sink. Then I was put back into the van and so was Felicity, who was now tied up as I was. The North Korean once again sat in the easy chair with his revolver, plus the Iranians on the floor. I saw that there was now a white man, in the driver's seat. I was still unable to read my watch on my roped wrist – my hands were tied behind my back – but from the sun I had read that it was very early morning when I'd been brought up from the well and the breakfast had been hasty. The roads should be empty enough for the van to have a good clear run for a while and presumably it was in no way a marked vehicle. I tried to talk to Felicity but was intercepted by the waving of the revolver under my nose.

"No talk," the North Korean said. So I didn't. I thought about Max and what interpretation he would be putting on my failure to report in. The body of the policeman in the Bradford funeral premises would have been found some while ago and Max would have put two and two together. My wonderings were about what action he would take. And what Whitehall would be doing.

I didn't even get any clues about that when the North Korean got up and slid open the window between us and the cab and jabbered at the driver and the radio was switched on. I heard the BBC's early morning news broadcast. There had been a shoot-up in Bradford. No mention of the move north of Al Kufra, of course, but the newsreader said that nothing further had been heard from the kidnappers and in the meantime the government was holding its hand, whatever that might be supposed to mean. It was all very bland and there was no reference to a second kidnap – me. The newsreader passed on to other matters. There had been an unconnected murder in Reading and a woman had been raped on the hard shoulder of the M1. Two nude bathers near Littlehampton in West Sussex had had their clothing nicked and had nakedly telephoned the police from a callbox . . .

The set was switched off.

After a while the van stopped, but only briefly. The men could have been consulting a road atlas. It moved on again, stopped again after a mile or so and another man joined the party. The window was still open and I heard him talking broad Scots. So we could be heading farther north. He had a loud voice and in the verbal exchanges I elucidated that he had joined by appointment and was going to act as guide; but I didn't get where to. I doubted if the destination would be too far north; if anything had by some mischance become known about the van the villains might find the Forth road bridge rather too much of a bottleneck for total safety. Then I remembered that they could go round by the motorway network outside Glasgow. And on to Stirling.

So I was none the wiser.

We stopped for petrol.

In the back, the guns moved in close and whispers told us both that they would be used if necessary. They were silenced but silencers aren't all that effective. The threat could have been an empty one but I wasn't prepared to risk Felicity's life. A better chance would come. The tank filled, we set off again. From the outside there was nothing to arouse anyone's suspicions. When we'd been embarked outside the farmhouse I'd seen the legend on sides and back: Ron Smith's Self-Drive Van Hire and a York telephone number. Very innocuous. Someone was moving house, perhaps, if anyone bothered to give the van a second glance and a little thought.

When finally we did stop, I had no idea in the world where it was, but I did know we had gone a very long way. Our ankles were freed and we were taken out in darkness and in rain and wind. Around me I saw the walls of a yard, and a building. That was all. We were taken through a door, no lights, anyway not till the door had been shut behind us. Then a light came on: we were in a warehouse and I saw what

57

looked like animal hides, great stacks of them, with an unpleasant smell.

"Move ahead, please," the Korean said. He shepherded us along a sort of alley between the hide stacks that rose almost to the roof. Near the alley's end we were turned to the right.

"Wait, please." We waited. One of the Iranians pushed past and disappeared behind the hides. Half a minute later there was the low sound of electrically operated machinery and just ahead of us one of the stacks moved out slowly across the alley between.

It left a hatch cover exposed.

The Iranian, switching off the power, came back to join us. He bent to the cover and lifted it away, exposing a hole around two feet square. He reached down inside, lying on the floor to extend his reach, and a light came on below. I saw a steep ladder with metal treads. The Iranian freed our wrists.

"Go down, please," the Korean said.

Felicity went first, then me, then the Oriental, then the rest of the party – all except the white van driver who had remained in his cab. I guessed he would be taking the van away from the scene, maybe disposing of it for good and all, a prudent safety precaution.

Once down the hole, with the hatch still open, we found ourselves in what looked at first sight like a set of offices, though in fact they could scarcely have been that. There was a long corridor, concrete floored, lined and ceilinged. Heavy doors, very heavy doors, opened off. The place smelled musty. We were pushed ahead of the guns along this passageway. Each door had a glass oblong, a spy-hole with wire reinforcements and barred. I caught glimpses of more merchandise – not hides, but crates. We were halted by two doors, which were unlocked and opened by one of the Iranians. Each compartment was empty, totally bare. One for me, one for Felicity. We were pushed in and the doors were locked.

The men moved away, back towards the hatch. I listened to their footsteps, growing fainter. Then the lights went out. The hatch banged back into place. Over it, no doubt, the great stack of hides would be moved back.

58

*

The darkness was intense. It was absolutely total, the blackest of black nights. There was also utter silence. It hovered on being unnerving. I had to fight down the feeling of panic: I breathed deeply, many times. It was almost like being in a coffin, one with room to move, one that would not kill mercifully by excluding air. There *was* air, if not fresh: a canned mustiness. My heart went out to Felicity next door to me. Next door, so close, but she might as well have been on the moon. The silence . . . then I heard the faint sound. A tapping, followed by a distant whisper, a whisper or a whistle, that seemed to come from the corner of the compartment, farthest from the door and on Felicity's side.

I went for the corner. I felt around. I found what felt like some sort of drain, or air brick maybe – anyway, there was a declivity and the whistle was coming from it.

I got down on my stomach and put my ear as close to the corner as I could and gave a low whistle back. I said, "Felicity."

"Yes."

"Are you all right?"

"Yes," she said in a shaky voice.

"Bear up," I whispered back. "We won't be left here for ever."

"I know. I just wanted to – to pass on something I overheard. When I was in the coffin and the drug had worn off enough for me to – "

"All right," I cut in. "I've got the picture. What's the message?"

She breathed just one word: "Tokushima."

Tokushima. That was all. In consternation and total surprise I asked, "You're sure? Quite sure?"

"Positive," she said. "Shaking . . . isn't it?"

"If it's still alive. Is it?"

"Yes," she said.

Tokushima. Now everything seemed to drop into place, the oriental involvement angle was explained. Tokushima had been the code name of an operation both Felicity and I had been co-ordinating some years before. We'd believed, Max had believed, Whitehall had believed that we'd bust it for good and all. It seemed we hadn't. A bunch of Japanese dissidents, Communists, in cahoots with a North Korean outfit supplying arms to certain terrorist organisations in Italy, France and Germany and also in Northern Ireland – the IRA and INLA. The big boss behind it had killed himself when we closed in and he'd almost killed me. I'd been hospitalised for a month afterwards. We'd got the others, or anyway most of them. But like the phoenix, a dedicated outfit could always rise again.

I whispered back to Felicity, asking if she'd picked up anything else.

"No," she said.

"No more talking now," I told her. It was better that way, just in case of bugs. But it was comforting to know that we could communicate if necessary. The loneliness was lessened quite considerably even though there was nothing positive we could do about our current situation. That, however, as I'd said to Felicity, wouldn't last. There would be contact with the villains sooner or later and I would just have to take it from there. In the meantime I thought about those crates I'd glimpsed through the small barred windows of the other underground compartments. Arms? Probably, if Tokushima was back in business.

And their purpose this time? We were, I still believed, in the north, maybe not far from the Clyde. Belfast lay across the North Channel, not so far from Ailsa Craig – we could even be in Glasgow itself, or some other Clydeside conurbation where there would be plenty of warehouses. There could, once again, be some link with the IRA. That began to seem the most likely. Max would be intensely interested. A different complexion was being put on the activities of the Friends of Al Kufra now. And I began to think the authorities had maybe played right into their hands by transferring Al Kufra to Stirling Castle, not so far from where we were being held if my guess was right. And closer, in all likelihood, to the arms possibly supplied by the Tokushima boys. I thought around it

60

all, trying to find the link. I doubted if the IRA would have any interest in Al Kufra or whether he was released or not. My mind travelled in circles, uselessly. I was physically pretty tired and things just were not working as they should and the air was close and foetid, not conducive to any clarity of thought.

At intervals food was brought, just enough to keep us alive, and water. Also at intervals I was taken under guard of two of the Iranians to a washroom with lavatory. I didn't know how long all this went on; there was no daylight to tell when day merged into night and vice versa. I spoke now and again through the wall to Felicity, just to keep our mutual spirits up. There had been no reaction to our initial whispered conversation so I was no longer too worried about bugs. I wished urgently for news of the world up top, but when the guards came with food and water and for ablutions they kept a deadly silence that I couldn't break. I wondered about the threat to Felicity's finger. After the cutting session had been broken up by the RAF over the north of England there had been no further attempt but I knew this could come and would. It was no more likely now than it had ever been that the Friends of Al Kufra would make empty threats.

Which was basically why I decided I had to take a chance and fast. If it didn't come off, matters couldn't be made any worse than they were already.

So far as I could tell, the one chance I was going to get was when the guards came with food. Or when I was taken to the washroom. My hands were no longer tied, they had never put the ropes back on after we'd gone down the hatch from the warehouse – they would have seen no need. Presumably Felicity was equally unbound. The guards were armed, naturally. That was the chance I would have to take. I doubted if they would want to kill me, though. As ever, a dead hostage has lost his value.

61

6

When the guards looked through the spy-hole I said I wanted to go to the washroom.

As usual they didn't even say yes; there was just a nod and a jerk of a head. I exited behind the guns, watching for my chance as I went along the concrete passageway to the washroom and through the door. The washroom consisted of rows of basins with hot and cold taps, twenty in all. Behind them a row of ten cubicles. No-one except me, so far as I knew, ever used them. There was no current work-force and certainly on the way in, however long ago that might have been, there had been no-one around. The place had had an air of abandonment, though why any previous owners should have left their animal hides behind I couldn't work out. Maybe, I'd thought during my cogitations, the Friends of Al Kufra, or the Japanese/North Korean consortium we'd code named Tokushima, had bought up the stock. They would have access to plenty of money and it could have been good cover, anyway temporarily. For long enough, that was.

I went to one of the basins and sluiced water over hands and face. I dried myself with paper towels from the dispenser. The guards were standing back against the door, shut behind them on entry. They were relaxed, feeling secure enough. When I was dry I turned round and went towards one of the cubicles. I went in. I didn't lock the door. When I was inside I gave what I hoped was a convincing shout of alarm, then I stood back.

Running footsteps heralded an approach, and the door was pushed open. The man asked in English, his very first speech since our arrival, "What is the matter?"

"This," I said, and got an arm in a tight lock round his neck, very fast. With my other hand I wrenched his gun-arm round and pointed his gun, which was silenced, into his stomach. By this time the second man was close. I said, "Hold it, or your friend commits suicide," and a moment later that was just what he did, by a possibly enforced pressure of his trigger-finger. Blood spurted, a lot of it going over me. But I had now got hold of the revolver and when the other man came for me I used it a fraction of a second before he used his own. He went down with a bullet through his throat and there was more spurting blood.

After that I wasted no time at all. I gathered up the second revolver and removed a big key from the belt of the first corpse, trusting that it would turn the lock of Felicity's cell, then I left the scene, dripping Iranian blood, and went fast to try the key. It was the one I wanted. The passage lights were still on and when I unlocked her door Felicity saw me and gave a gasp of unbelieving astonishment.

"What – "

"No time," I said. "Just keep close to me. We're going to take another chance and we have to be bloody fast."

"Where do you – "

"We go for the hatch," I said. "It'll still be open. Or we hope so. Come on!"

She didn't say any more. I gave her one of the revolvers. I ran along the passage and she came behind, keeping close as ordered. I reached the ladder and found the hatch still open as expected. I went up the ladder fast. The lights were on up top as well as below and I paused to take a look around. There was no sign of life. Currently we were shielded by the great stacks of animal hides. There was silence, though from the distance I heard what I took to be traffic sounds. The lights being on, I was as yet unable to see if it was daylight outside or not. If there were windows, they were invisible behind the tall hide stacks.

I came through the hatch with my borrowed revolver ready, and gestured to Felicity to do likewise. We moved silently

63

along the alley formed by the hide stacks, and turned into the main alley that ran through to the big doors at the end. There was still no-one around. We moved fast and on reaching the doors found them locked, a big bar running across, hinged at one end, padlocked at the other.

I looked around.

There was no other way out that I could see.

"What now?" Felicity asked. She was white and her face was pinched, deep shadows beneath the eyes, and she was trembling. "They'll get us – "

"It's time," I said, "to wake the dead and take another chance." It was all I could do anyway. I told Felicity to stand back and I put the barrel of the Iranian's revolver against the padlock and squeezed the trigger. Two bullets did the job. Silenced or not, there was more noise than I liked. I lifted the bar clear and swung the doors open and we moved out into the warehouse yard. The gates stood open and there was a van, not the van we'd come north in, and two men who had been working on it in the light of torches – it was night. I opened fire before they did, and one of them went down screaming, taking his mate with him as he fell, which gave us our chance. We were through the gate and running down a sleazy road with few street lights before the second man had recovered himself. The wounded man went on screaming and bullets came from behind us. We pelted on: all things considered, Felicity made good speed. I turned into the first side road we came to, and ran on. We came then to a cluster of long, low buildings that looked like a more modern industrial estate than the warehouse we had left. Beyond this again there were what had been slum tenements, very tall, very grim and grimy. They stretched ahead out of sight. They had the feeling of a long-gone Glasgow, something like the Gorbals.

"This'll do us," I said. The pursuit was still behind us and although the shooting had stopped, for the sake of prudence in a public place I supposed, the one man had now been re-inforced and I heard the pounding feet of a number of men. And they were closing: Felicity was getting breathless.

We turned into the tenements, entering through a broken-down doorway. Inside, the place was littered with debris, plaster, rotting woodwork, piles of stinking rubbish. Broken stone steps led upwards. The whole series of tenements was obviously awaiting demolition, the last piece, perhaps, of an old squalor.

"Up the stairs," I said. "Fast as you can."

We went up. There was graffiti on the bare walls, lurid statements and desires. The smell was of decay and urine and worse. It was a rabbit-warren; many of the interior walls had gaping holes and we progressed from one tenement to another, on and on, getting very nicely lost. In one passage-way we stumbled over a heap of rags and newspapers, and the heap moved to reveal a face that reflected moonlight coming through a hole in the wall. The eyes stared at us but didn't see us; a hand clasped, with a grip like death, a half-empty bottle of methylated spirits. The air was thick: strike a match and he'd have gone up like a bomb.

Sounds came from somewhere below. "They're coming up," Felicity said.

I moved through another hole in a wall and came to a landing. Stone stairs led up and down. I said, "We'll take up a defensive position here. Get 'em as they come up."

I had only one round left in the chambers and no spare ammunition. Felicity's gun had five bullets. I reckoned we were going to need them all, but I was wrong. Sounds play funny tricks at times; their whereabouts are hard to pin-point. No-one came up our stairs.

"It's all right," I said. "For now, anyway. We just keep dead quiet. And do a lot of praying. All right?"

She nodded, her face taut in the moon's light. I took her in my arms and held her close. She was still shivering, not just from the cold of the derelict tenements, but I think I gave her some comfort. The sounds continued and then seemed to be coming closer. Inactivity, keeping quiet, could go on a shade too long. I said, "We'll have to shift, Felicity."

We shifted, taking it slowly and carefully, hoping not to dislodge any debris. We came upon more recumbent forms, and one not so recumbent who shook and cried out, something

65

unintelligible in a female voice. It sounded like curses, accompanied by a waved fist. We moved on. Before much longer we would come, I believed, to the final wall, the slab side of the last tenement, after which we would be able to move only up or down. No help would come. Only the down-and-outs moved here and probably the police didn't penetrate in the normal course of events, leaving some sort of refuge for the despairing homeless, the rough sleepers.

We did come to that final wall. A blankness in stone and concrete, still standing. I looked upwards, feeling raindrops. The floors above us had collapsed to block the upward-leading stairs, and this section was roofless and I saw the sky reflecting distant town lights, and the rainclouds.

"Here we stick," I said.

"How long?"

"Let's just wait and see what happens next," I said.

It was very cold now. We were able to move back out of the rain but there was nothing to be done about the cold. We waited for what seemed a very long time, hearing those sounds of search from below and to one side, the side we had come from, before they diminished and then stopped. I thought about trying to find some way out to the rear, which I had noted earlier from a hole that served as a window to be open ground filled with lumps of stone and concrete and broken-down privies. There would be cover, scattered cover anyway, and beyond I'd seen a river, probably the Clyde on its course through Glasgow, if we were in Glasgow, and somehow the tenement had the feel of Glasgow, and the female voice had had the Gorbals unintelligibility, to a Sassenach anyway.

When there had been no sound for a long while, I decided, for good or ill, to move down. There was an obvious urgency to reach a telephone, to get a police cordon round the warehouse, to make arrests while there was still time. I didn't expect our villains to hang around till daylight. They could make their getaway even if they had to leave their armoury – if that was what was in the crates – behind. The Japanese connection would find it easy enough, probably, to make up the deficiency.

66

We moved down. There were still no sounds. Down to the next landing, and the next, and the next. No opposition. We had reached ground level when I heard movement, a sort of scrabbling as though debris was being disturbed. I put a hand on Felicity's arm and we froze. I took her revolver, the one with the five rounds in the chambers, and I cocked it.

A dog appeared in a patch of light from the street. A mangy, scavenging dog. I stared at it.

Then it began barking, loudly, angrily, and its hackles came up. The jaws slavered, the barking continued. It didn't intend to stop. Too late now for doggy talk in an attempt to get on terms and prove we loved it, that we were just friends.

The damage had been done.

I saw the dark-skinned man come round the angle of a wall and I saw him go into a crouch and bring up his gun. We both fired together. His shot skimmed my left arm, though I wasn't aware of it at the time. Mine got him between the eyes and he keeled over, head asunder and face invisible behind the blood. Then it all happened with shattering suddenness.

Maybe it had been the gunfire: I just don't know. I didn't even know quite what happened, or anyway the exact sequence of events. But the result was that the part of the building we had been in collapsed, the very ground opening beneath us as the end wall went – outwards, fortunately. We were both knocked cold; not for all that long as I assessed later. When we came round it was in darkness still and there was a slop of water around us. My head ached and I was sore and stiff all over, but I was alive at any rate. It had been something of a miracle and we probably owed our salvation to the stone staircase, much as in the wartime days the safest place from bombs was said to be beneath the stairs. We had been beneath the risers when the shooting had taken place.

I was able to move, just a little. I reached out and contacted Felicity. I spoke to her; she answered. The relief was immense. I asked her if she could move.

There was a pause. "Limbs okay," she said, "but there's not much room, is there?"

"Restricted," I agreed.

"D'you think more will come down?"

Frankly, I thought it more than possible. But I said, trying to be reassuring, "I doubt it. That one shift'll have settled it all into a new position. I'm not worried."

"How about getting out?"

"Wait a while," I said. "That business of settling . . . if we try to shift anything, then more *could* come down."

"Wait for rescue?" she asked.

"Yes. Like the war. The heavy rescue squads. They'll soon know there's been a collapse, and they'll know the down-and-outs use this building. They'll be along."

"And the men from the warehouse?"

I laughed, not a very humorous sound. "With any luck, they'll write us off now." I didn't really believe that; if the whole building had gone, then perhaps they would have come to that conclusion, but I reckoned it must be only a small part that had been affected.

So we waited, there being nothing else to be done about it. Just wait and think all manner of thoughts. I had already briefly asked Felicity about her treatment since the kidnap. She said she'd spent most of the time drugged, in the coffin, but at the other times there had been no ill-treatment as such. I had asked if she'd recognised any of the men and she hadn't, any more than I had with the exception of Safi Suduteh now known as Behzad Habibi. And she hadn't heard much about the Tokushima operation, just enough to convince her that it was once again on the march. It had just been a chance remark, in English: the Iranians and the North Korean had no other shared language. It hadn't been very revealing; just a few words to say that Kyoshiro Ka was being very helpful. Kyoshiro Ka had been one of the big-boy Japanese arms runners involved in Tokushima, the Number Two we had never got our hands on. If Kyoshiro Ka was active again, then undoubtedly what had been represented by the code name Tokushima was alive and kicking. And I had to find out what they were after this time. I still found it hard to believe they were concerned about Al Kufra and his fate.

Currently I could do nothing about anything. I talked to Felicity, trying to keep her mind occupied. After a while a streak of daylight showed through from somewhere and as it strengthened I was able to see our surroundings. Broken concrete, and that water in which we were lying and growing colder and colder. It was only around two inches deep, but that was bad enough and I fancied after a while that it was very slowly deepening.

Then, at long last, the sounds from the world beyond our concrete prison, the shouts of men and the rumble of heavy equipment. I called out, and after calling for some while I was answered. The accent was Scots and it was reassuring. It would take time, the voice called. Much care was going to be necessary, but we would be brought out.

He wasn't wrong: it took time, a lot of time. They weren't going to rush anything. A lot of broken masonry had to be lifted clear by a crane before they could begin to work down towards us.

I'd asked, soon after some sort of communication had been established, to speak to a police officer. An inspector had answered the call. I said I wanted a warehouse surrounded and checked out and he was very sceptical.

"Who are you?" he called down. I believe he thought I was one of the rough sleepers, a natural enough presumption in the circumstances.

"Have you heard of 6D2?" I asked.

"I have not, no."

"Contact your HQ," I said. "Someone there will know. The name's Shaw. It's urgent, believe me."

"Oh, aye." The tone was utterly disbelieving. "This warehouse, now. Where is it?"

I gave directions, back along the route we'd run the night before. The inspector seemed to latch on. "The skins," I heard him say, addressing someone else, probably his sergeant. "New people just recently." That was all; no more talk. He'd gone away – to call up his HQ on a car's radio, I hoped. But he didn't come back and we went on waiting for the heavy rescue boys to dig down and through. Which at last they did, and lifted us clear. I asked to be taken straight to police HQ, but first they put a medic onto us, to see if hospital wasn't the proper destination. I did a certain amount of insisting and rather grudgingly the doctor said I was in pretty fair shape considering. But he wouldn't play ball with Felicity: she had a lump on the back of her head and they put her in an ambulance to be taken to casualty for incarceration overnight at least.

I spoke to the inspector, this time face to face. He was a very dour Scot indeed, horse-faced and sardonic. I asked him if he'd reported in as requested.

"Aye," he said.

"And the warehouse?"

"Oh, aye, we checked."

"And?" I wanted to shake it out of him, but saw clearly that a show of impatience would rile him. He didn't like Sassenachs.

"Nothing," he said. "Or not much."

"For Christ's sake," I said, unable to keep it back.

"There's no need for blasphemy, now." He became a little more expansive. "There were the hides, yes."

"Down below?"

"Down below there was also nothing. No persons – "

"The crates – "

"Aye, there were crates, yes, a number of them. All empty."

"Empty," I repeated dully. "And no persons."

"No persons. Much blood in various places. And three bodies. *Dead* bodies." He rose and fell on the balls of his feet. I thought: three? The wounded man must have pegged out. "You may be who you say you are, Mr Shaw, and as to that, time will tell. In the meantime you have admitted having come from a place where there are dead bodies upon whom guns have been used and you have arms on your person. There will be questions to be answered at the station. If you don't mind."

"Do I take it I'm being arrested?"

70

"Aye," he said complacently, smiling for the first time. "That looks to be the way of it."

It was raining now and I was wet already from lying in that slop of water. The sooner this was all sorted out the better for everyone. I was put into the back of a police car, the inspector got in beside the driver and we left the scene. I was very far from happy, seeing that the birds had flown. And empty crates? What did that mean? That they'd been empty all along, the warehouse *not* being the arms dump? Or that they'd flown and taken the contents of the crates with them? I thought, not the latter. They'd have taken the crates for fast loading into the van, surely.

I was back to the beginning again.

At the station, I told the whole story. More or less. No secrets revealed. Just the bare facts. I had shot the men, I said, because Felicity and I were being held captive under threat. And I had a job to do.

"For 6D2?" the chief superintendent in charge asked.

"Yes. You know about 6D2?"

"I do, yes. And I've contacted your HQ. You've been vouched for, Commander Shaw."

"I'm glad to hear it. Charges?"

"No charges," he said with obvious regret. "Your bloody people . . . but I'll not let off steam now." A lot of the police didn't like 6D2, didn't like our powers, didn't like our being in so many respects beyond the law's reach – a good deal of it was jealousy pure and simple, of course. The chief superintendent went on, "You'll have heard the warehouse was empty but for the animal hides – "

"If someone had been a shade faster," I said bitterly, "it just might not have been."

"The word of someone who might very well have been on the meths needed checking out before we could act. That should be obvious, Commander Shaw. We can't go blustering into private property on the word of a bum, and to repeat myself, you could have been a bum."

"All right," I said. "I could have been a bum but wasn't.

71

Let's leave it at that. Now will you please put me in touch with Focal House?"

This was arranged. I spoke after some delay to Max, on the security line. I gave a brief report, the bare essentials, and I told him what Felicity had picked up about Tokushima. Max didn't like that at all. I was ordered to report in person soonest possible. There had been some political stirrings and Max was having trouble with a man named Spatchcock from the Foreign Office. Miss Mandrake, Max said, would have to be left in hospital meanwhile; I'd already told him there was a police presence at her bedside – she was in a private room, or anyway a private cubicle, I'd been informed.

So I was driven to the airport and a plane for London, wondering where the trail would lead next. Or if it would lead anywhere. It seemed to have gone cold already.

Max had dug out the gone-cold file on Tokushima but it didn't add much. I had all the facts at my fingertips already. I asked Max what he thought about the apparent connection between the Friends of Al Kufra and the arms suppliers.

He shrugged. "Clear as mud, Shaw. I doubt if the idea's to· blow up Stirling Castle!"

"With Al Kufra *in situ*."

"What?" He looked at me sharply; my tone had been thoughtful.

I said, "It wouldn't be a very friendly act. But perhaps friendship doesn't come into it. Perhaps the Friends of Al Kufra are just being made use of."

"By Kyoshiro Ka?"

I nodded. "Could be. Just an idea."

"Which leads us where?"

"I don't know," I said, still thoughtful. "A dirty game – but then it always is. I'm thinking along the lines of a possible IRA involvement, Max. Blowups being their speciality. Especially of military targets."

Max frowned. "You're seriously considering something at Stirling?"

"Perhaps. I say again, it's just an idea – " I broke off; Max's internal telephone was burring. I heard the voice of Mrs Dodge, his personal secretary. Mr Spatchcock, it seemed – the man with whom Max had been having trouble – was in the secretary's office; he hadn't been expected, and Max swore, but told Mrs Dodge to bring him in. Putting down the telephone with a bang, he told me Spatchcock was some sort of under-secretary in the Foreign Office and a bloody nuisance to boot. His full name was a marvel: Hubert Murlees Egremont Spatchcock. When Spatchcock was ushered in I saw something that I'd thought went out with the Attlee era. Black coat, striped trousers, even spats of all things, hanging on the bony frame of a very tall, thin man with a long face, wearing gold pince-nez and a hearing aid.

I was introduced to Mr Spatchcock, who gave me a distant look full of disapproval, a look that travelled down his nose as he held his head back.

"Ah, Commander Shaw. I've heard of you. Yes."

There seemed to be no reply to that. Max gestured Spatchcock to a chair and the long body diminished into out-thrust legs and hands held in front of the face, the fingertips touching in a parsonic gesture. Spatchcock cleared his throat. "Very good of you to see me at such short notice. A nasty business, all this. The PM's upset, you know."

Max said, "Yes, I do know. I've been in touch."

The eyebrows met. "Not personally – do you mean?"

"Yes, personally."

"H'm." There was disapproval again but it was not put into words. Or not very precisely. "I don't think . . . but never mind, never mind. The thing is, we can't concede. Certainly not that. Certainly not."

"I agree," Max said.

"On the other hand there are various interests to be considered."

"Such as?"

Spatchcock wasn't going to commit himself too far, I thought. He didn't. He cleared his throat again and answered Max obliquely, "I understand the hostage has been freed."

Max waved a hand towards me. "Correct. By Shaw here.

You'll have had the reports from the police in Glasgow, of course."

"Yes, indeed. Indeed, yes. What I'm getting at is this: the way is clearer now that there is no hostage – "

"Clearer for what, Mr Spatchcock?"

"Shall we say . . . for the various interests to which I made reference just now. In my view, you see, it's largely a matter of *face*. Now that the hostage has been freed, these people can make no more threats in that direction. Naturally, no responsible government can ever give in to threat, to blackmail of that sort. That goes without saying. But in the new circumstances there may well be room for manoeuvre."

Max's jaw came out belligerently. "I see no room for manoeuvre at all, if by manoeuvre you mean compromise, Mr Spatchcock. As I rather think you do. Either Al Kufra is handed over or he is not. Agreed?"

"Oh, yes, indeed. Yes, I do agree so far as it goes. But don't you see . . . Al Kufra himself could become a bargaining counter. His release is being demanded, is it not, by Iranian nationals?"

"Libyan, actually," I said.

"Yes, yes. I thought I said Libyan. But . . ." Spatchcock cleared his throat again and leaned forward a little in his chair. "Libya, yes. But there are matters between ourselves and the Iranian Government in Teheran, and both Libya and Iran are in cahoots . . . important matters, as of course you'll be very aware."

"Oil?"

Spatchcock nodded. "Oil, yes, certainly. Perhaps more importantly, a need to improve relations . . . largely in order to keep out Soviet influence."

Max said just one word: "*Glasnost.*"

"Ah, yes, *glasnost* indeed. Indeed, yes. A very different picture from a few years ago. We no longer *fear* the Soviets, of course. No longer. On the other hand, we have our interests to consider and to protect. HM Government has no wish to see any *expansion* of Soviet interests, *glasnost* or not. I think you will see that quite clearly?"

74

Max said, "I see one thing quite clearly and it's this: you're saying that Whitehall might consider releasing Al Kufra if there was advantage to be gained from so doing. Releasing a killer, Mr Spatchcock. It's not just his past outrages. Police officers have died in the last few days as a result of the activities of the so-called Friends of Al Kufra. You suggest releasing such a man, in all seriousness?"

"*I* do not. It would not be *my* decision, nor that of the Foreign Secretary. It would be a collective decision by the cabinet. Though of course the Secretary of State's advice would be paramount and likely to be much heeded. Much heeded. His and the Home Secretary's. On the other hand . . ."

"Yes, Mr Spatchcock?"

"There are other ways." Spatchcock closed his eyes for a moment.

"Really." Max was glowering. "I'd be obliged if you'd tell me precisely why you've come to us, to Focal House, with this – this suggestion? 6D2 is not the government, Mr Spatchcock. We don't make policy decisions. We are simply an agency – that's all. So why?"

Spatchcock once again cleared his throat. "You've put it in a nutshell," he said. "It is *because* you are an agency. You can be of very great service. If your organisation will conduct any necessary negotiations . . . well, then Whitehall can keep clear of – of – "

"Opprobrium?" Max suggested nastily.

"A hard word, but I believe you have taken my point," Spatchcock said. He looked at his watch and got to his feet. "I have an appointment at the Cabinet Office," he said. "Thank you so much for seeing me."

He took his departure and left Max and me staring at each other in a mixture of anger and incredulity.

7

"Fowl killed and cooked in a hurry," Max said. He was looking livid. "Or insert words hastily in a telegram – that's a colloquialism."

I stared at him. "I don't get it," I said.

"Spatchcock. I'm quoting the Concise Oxford Dictionary . . . I looked it up earlier. Bloody man! They're all the same in Whitehall, of course."

An exaggeration but one with much truth in it. Spatchcock had been imprecise as was perhaps to be expected of a permanent civil servant and especially a highly-placed one, an under-secretary of state who had to watch his step twenty-four hours a day. But what he was suggesting – what he hadn't actually said – was as clear as the Lutine Bell at Lloyd's. We both knew it. 6D2 was being asked to conduct negotiations behind the scenes with the authorities, or more probably their anonymous nominees to coin a doubtful phrase, in Teheran; negotiations aimed at the release of Al Kufra in exchange for advantages not specifically spelled out.

"Release my foot," Max said savagely, bringing a heavy fist down on his expensive tulip-wood desk. "Absolute cock – or Spatchcock!"

I understood without further word from Max: release would quite obviously, as Max had said to Spatchcock, have to be as a result of a government order, not an order from 6D2 whose fiat didn't run to those sort of heights. And equally obviously Spatchcock had meant it when he'd said there could be no question of conceding. There were all those other governments – USA, France, Germany, Italy – who would be quite rightly scandalised.

No, there would be no *release* of Al Kufra. Absolutely none. The British Government would stand firm, four square to threat and blackmail and Middle Eastern terrorism. Al Kufra, Spatchcock hadn't said but meant, could be allowed to escape. And 6D2 was to be the intermediary via the secret negotiations in Teheran.

Max detested it, I knew; but he put in a word of wisdom, the sort of wisdom employed by governments when there was something to be gained. He said, "It's one way of getting rid of an embarrassment, you know. This attempt – the Friends of Al Kufra – may well fail. It must, of course. Fail *as such*. But it'll come up again and again for so long as Al Kufra's held in jail. And more people will die. There will be more hostages. What Spatchcock is offering, or what he's been ordered to offer in the never-to-be-revealed name of someone higher up, someone in the cabinet perhaps, is a way out without surrender. A way out for all time."

"You're as bad as Spatchcock," I said bitterly. "With respect, of course."

"You must look at it logically, Shaw."

"Through a fouled-up glass. Do I take it you're going along with Spatchcock, then?"

Max compromised. "We'll see which way the wind is blowing first."

"Meaning what, exactly?"

Max shrugged heavily. He was looking tired, I thought; he wasn't young. Maybe the brain was softening. He said, "It means what it says. I have to say this – you've not produced much yet. I'm not casting blame. You've had a hard time just recently. And it was the police who let the birds get away by their delay – I know all that. But turn something more up – and then we'll see. But you'll have to move fast."

There had been a degree of unusual dither about Max that day; he was a worried man. So was I. There was really nothing to go on. Up north in the Glasgow nick I'd been told that the previous owners of that warehouse had been a firm called Nexolite Leathers (Glasgow and Edinburgh) plc. Their business had been import and export – import, presumably, of the raw hides, export after they'd been treated or whatever, made into saleable leather. This, I told Max for what it was worth, adding that the Glasgow police were making enquiries into the firm which they believed had gone out of business altogether so enquiries might take time. I went back to the suggestion of an escape, asking who would be supposed to organise that. I said that perhaps some unfortunate prison governor and his staff could be coerced and rewarded later with golden handshakes.

"Balls," he said forcefully. "That's not the way things are done – "

"Aren't they?"

He grinned at my tone. "They might be, I suppose, if it wasn't for the fact that too many people would have to be privy to it. But you're forgetting one thing, aren't you?"

"What?"

"Stirling Castle. It's not an official prison. Doesn't come under the Prisons Department. Or the Director of the Scottish Prison Service in Edinburgh."

"So that's why Al Kufra wasn't transferred to somewhere like Barlinnie?"

"It's likely."

"In other words, it's been in Whitehall's mind from the start, the escape idea?"

"I'd say that's a fair summary," Max said. He went on to talk about Stirling Castle. It was a secure enough place, or had been, anyway from a military viewpoint. There was a presence of the army, in the form of the Argyll and Sutherland Highlanders and the cadet training teams – the Argylls had their HQ mess there, and the regimental museum, and the regimental chapel; but of course it had not been designed as a prison. Also, there were a number of civilians working in the castle – any 'escape' from there could be much more easily covered up than from, say, Barlinnie, or Perth, or Peterhead – or any prison south of the border, too. The more I thought about it after that session with Max and Spatchcock, the more

I thought Whitehall had been set all along on the escape idea, just so long as Teheran could be persuaded to come up with something good. And I went on to think that their nasty plans could well be upset, scattered wholesale, now that Tokushima had come back into the picture. I put this to Max.

"Yes," he said. "Your views about the IRA involvement – I know. But look at it another way: suppose the IRA *is* involved, along with Kyoshiro Ka. Say, an attack with high explosives on Stirling Castle. For the IRA, a very prestigious target indeed. Military – and in mainland Britain."

"And the escape – "

"Under cover of an IRA attack. So we *do* come back to that after all. As a theory to work on, anyway."

"But not," I said, making the point a second time, "with Al Kufra inside." I paused. "I suppose they could dig him out first." Then I paused again; I'd had the thought that the Al Kufra rescue brigade was merely being made use of. Al Kufra *could* get caught in the blowup and the IRA wouldn't care less. Max, it seemed, had guessed the way my thoughts were going.

He said, "The situation has to be resolved before Tokushima takes off again. If Al Kufra leaves this world before anything's been achieved in Teheran – "

"So you really are going along with that?"

He said yes, he was. For the time being, anyway. It would do no harm to send a man to Teheran for at least preliminary discussions, to feel his way around. 6D2 Britain's top Middle Eastern negotiator, Brian Horley, would be sent in right away. And in the meantime, Max would have words with Defence Ministry and the Scottish Office about possible explosions in Stirling.

I had a session with Brian Horley, filling him in on recent events and giving him a full briefing on the past activities of Kyoshiro Ka and his confederates and on the whole of Operation Tokushima. That done, I went back north to where the action currently was. I went by Inter City because I needed sleep and Inter City travel would give me the best chance of that. After an early, snatched lunch in the 6D2 dining-room I left Euston in a first-class compartment, and was flaked out asleep by the time the express had passed through the outer London suburbs. Before drifting off I'd had a perhaps unworthy thought: the reason Max was being so compliant with the ideas of the wretched Spatchcock might be connected with the massive government grant made available annually to 6D2 Britain without overtly appearing on the Treasury's requisition. But if so, then that really wouldn't be much like the Max I'd known for so many years of service.

The Inter City stopped at Crewe and I woke up. A number of people got out; I watched them walking along the platform, carrying hand luggage. Another lot boarded, some of them entering my coach. A girl seated herself diagonally across the gangway from me, to my right, her back to the engine. She was young and attractive, casually dressed in cords and a loose anorak-type garment. Long dark hair. She brought a magazine from a bag and began reading as the Inter City got under way again, pulling out fast for Carlisle and Glasgow. I went back to sleep and woke again at Carlisle. A man got in and sat alongside the girl, who gave him a glance and shifted herself nearer the window. She had stopped reading; she just sat, looking out as the Inter City pulled on past the castle. Another place with a military presence still, regimental headquarters of the King's Own Royal Border Regiment. The man who had got in was a rough sort; flashy clothes and a big gold ring on the third finger of his right hand, a ring with an overlarge lapis lazuli in it. He kept giving the girl sideways looks, but she kept her face turned away. I went back to sleep.

It was evening, just before 8 p.m., when the Inter City pulled in to Glasgow Central. Passengers streamed down the platform. I saw the girl for a while then lost her. Outside the station, I took a taxi to police HQ. I asked the duty inspector if anything had come to hand, and I asked about Felicity.

"The lady's doing fine," he told me. "She'll no doubt be discharged after consultant's rounds in the morning. Aside from that, there's nothing to report."

"Nothing on Nexolite Leathers?"

"Nothing doing in that direction."

"They have gone out of business, then? You've confirmed that, have you?"

He nodded. "Aye, we have. We've contacted all the directors . . . they're in the clear. They sold the entire stock to the newcomers. They were a family firm, not large, three brothers and a cousin, all of them elderly."

"Retired?"

"Aye, retired now."

"And the newcomers?"

The inspector leafed through some papers on his desk. "A firm called MegaWorld, all one word."

"Anything known?"

"Not a thing. The name doesn't appear in any of the usual lists of such. It's my opinion it never existed at all. There's just one thing of possible interest: the late directors of Nexolite Leathers said the men they negotiated with were from the Middle East – "

"I don't doubt it," I said. "Any names?"

"Aye." The inspector showed me the names on the file. None of them meant anything to me, though I recognised them as being probably Iranian names, though it was hard to be dead certain. The inspector added, "They could all be aliases, and likely are."

I agreed with that. I said, "You'll be carrying on the investigation, I take it?"

"Oh, aye. We'll be carrying on." He didn't sound very interested or very hopeful. "What do you propose to do now, Commander Shaw?"

I shrugged. "Take a look around," I said.

"Where?"

"Just – Glasgow. I may pay a visit to the warehouse. Or I may not."

"You'd best watch it," he advised. "We don't want another kidnap. Or another tenement falling down. Do we?" He regarded me with a weary and sardonic look: I was being a bloody nuisance to the police, that look said quite clearly. I sympathised; I was often a nuisance to the official boys. And the inspector, like the late board of directors of Nexolite

Leathers, was no longer young. Nearing retirement, maybe hopes of promotion gone, he no doubt liked a quiet life and I didn't blame him. But I was allowed no quiet life; it was all slog.

I drifted around the city, beneath the city lights. Sauchiehall Street, George Square, Queen Street . . . there were plenty of people around, many of them lurching drunk. It wasn't Saturday night, it was Friday, but that hadn't deterred the determined boozers of the north. Later, many pubs were still open and men were being urged out, some of them forcibly. There was song in the air, and from somewhere I heard the skirl of the pipes, a rather amateur effort that faded into the sounds of raucous laughter and then yells as a fight developed. I had only a vague idea of what I was looking for: any dark skins, any known faces, in particular Safi Suduteh alias Behzad Habibi. Or an Oriental, with luck. I was not very expectant; but there is always a lot to be said for chance.

No luck this time, however. I thought about the warehouse. I had an urge to have a look around for myself; the police do miss things now and again. The night held its dangers, as I was well aware, especially in Glasgow. Glasgow had always had a reputation for toughness and there was no reason to suppose things had changed now that there was more affluence around; there was high unemployment on the Clyde still, so the affluence wasn't all that terrific in fact.

I started for the warehouse. On foot, because I didn't want to turn up in a police car. The keynote was anonymity. It was a long way and though I knew the direction, and had once known Glasgow reasonably well, I got myself lost more than once; the geography had changed a good deal, so many of the old landmarks gone, whole streets simply vanished under the bulldozers and the directives of the town planners. It was a very different city now from what I'd known. Cleaner, less grim, but at the same time without character, soulless, high rise everywhere, looking like immense barrack blocks. Not many people about; they were mostly shut up in their barrack-rooms which may have been a very great improvement on the old tenement buildings with their closes and outside privies and the squalor, but I guessed that a lot of the neighbourliness would have gone, as it had gone elsewhere in Britain.

It was a lonely walk and one in which I kept my senses fully alert for trouble. And it wasn't long before I knew I had a tail. At first it was instinctive rather than anything more positive; I didn't get what I would call a sight of the tail. Just a shadowy figure now and again after a while, never where there was a street light, and after a while the street lights grew less in number anyway. I didn't increase my pace; nor did I look round, not right round; just a quick look whenever I crossed the road, that was all. There was a little traffic, not much. The long, long walk neared its end when I came to the derelict tenement where Felicity and I had spent the previous night. I saw again the collapsed part, saw that it had all been roped off and that there was a p.c. on duty there, no doubt to warn off the deadbeats who might have sought shelter for the night in their sacks and old newspapers.

I turned to stare at the collapse as any passer-by might. The constable looked back at me, taking no particular notice. I gave a quick glance towards where I'd come from, and I didn't see the tail anywhere, but had to assume it was there still, fading into the background. Or maybe it knew, now, that I was positively bound for the warehouse, and had pulled out to make contact with someone else. In which case I could be walking into a trap. Max would undoubtedly say I was being remarkably foolish. He could have been right. But something was nagging at me and I wanted, badly now, to take that close look around. For one thing, I didn't believe the police had been one hundred per cent thorough in their own search. I believed there could be arms around still. I still didn't believe the villains would have emptied out the cases and removed the arms loose as it were. It didn't add up, not quite.

I called goodnight to the constable.

"Goodnight then," he said amiably. "Going home, are you?"

"Yes," I said.

"I didna' think you were one of the rough sleepers." He wasn't one of the officers who'd been there when I was dug out; he didn't know me. I moved on, coming into shadow. Right down the front of the building until I was past the pool of light in which the policeman stood.

I moved deep into the shadow of the tenements, and I waited.

Someone came past the policeman. Goodnights were exchanged and I picked up a Northern Irish accent. Whoever it was came closer, into my range of vision, and in the loom of light from farther back I recognised the man who'd boarded the Inter City at Carlisle.

8

The man was looking to right and left and seemed hesitant. He was off his stroke, I suspected; he'd lost me but he had to keep moving because of the guarding copper at the collapsed end of the tenements. I saw collusion somewhere along the line – literally, along the railway line. Someone could have tailed me onto the train, then handed over to the girl at Crewe, who had handed over to the man boarding at Carlisle. Something like that, though I had no reason at all to suspect the girl and I had to admit it.

The man moved out of sight. I waited. He could be waiting too, or he might be going on to the warehouse. There was no knowing. I had two courses of action as possibilities: I could go back to the constable and get him to call HQ on his pocket transceiver and bring the fuzz in. I rejected that even before I'd properly formulated it in my mind: the man would see and would be flushed, and anyway I wanted that private look around. The second course of action was to come out from cover and walk on and deal with the tail myself if he closed in.

That was what I did. It was a risk but it was too soon for the police. I was much intrigued by that harsh Northern Irish accent that fitted with my theories about an IRA involvement. I could for all I knew be about to tangle with the IRA's Belfast Brigade. If there was that link with the Friends of Al Kufra, the IRA boyos would know all about me, that was certain.

The street was empty now, no sign of the man. It was an eerie progress towards the warehouse, the silent streets, the dereliction. There was the odd scavenging cat and once a demoniac shriek and much spitting as two cats met in mutual hostility. That was all.

I approached the warehouse gates, now shut and pad-locked. I reached up, got a grip, and heaved myself up to a sitting position on top, then jumped down the other side. Nothing moved. I brought out the automatic from my shoulder holster – I'd been re-equipped armswise in Focal House that morning. I had a powerful torch in my pocket. The doors into the warehouse loomed. There was no sign of the man. It was possible he'd given up, realising he'd been rumbled once I'd hauled off into the shadows by the tenements, and not liking the too close presence of that constable on watch. No police guard, I'd been told at the nick, had been left on the warehouse; once forensic and the photographers had finished they had simply replaced the gun-shattered pad-lock. I didn't propose to shoot out the new one. There were windows, almost opaque with accumulated dirt. I could probably gain entry without too much hassle.

I was approaching one of those windows when I heard the slight sound, a step on some uneven ground. I turned, fast, and saw the man very close, a revolver pointed at me. I ducked as he fired; the bullet nicked my sleeve and thudded into the wall behind and, powered by my leg muscles, I gave him a head-butt in the stomach and he went down gasping, winded so that it took him time to get his breath going again. I grabbed his revolver and waited for him to recover.

"You bastard," he said after a while.

He made to get up. "Stay put," I said. "And tell me who you are and why you've been tailing me."

He said, "Get stuffed." Then he added, "Who are you, anyway?"

I laughed. "As if you didn't know!"

"I *don't* know."

"So you usually aim to kill someone you don't know?"

"It's sometimes a personal reflex action," he said surlily, "but this time I was just aiming to immobilise – and I wasn't tailing anybody at all. I suggest you give that revolver back to me." He paused. "You don't talk like a villain. And you're not Irish. Just who are you?"

I was a shade disconcerted now. He didn't sound like a

villain either, though the flashy clothes and the ring as seen in the train were not reassuring. But you don't have to be a villain to dress like that. I said, "I seem to have the gun hand. I suggest you cough first. Then we'll see."

He muttered something I didn't catch. I had the torch on him by this time. He reached into his inside pocket and my finger tightened a little on the trigger of the revolver, another reflex action. But I needn't have bothered. He just brought out a wallet and pulled out a card. An identity card, which he handed to me.

He said, "CID. RUC."

"I'll be buggered," I said.

"You will be, friend, if you don't watch it. Who are you?"

I said, "The name's Shaw. 6D2."

He sighed. I let him get to his feet. He said, "So there's been a cock-up. It's not unusual, not at all unusual."

"But it's a bloody pity," I said, sounding savage. I felt savage, very savage. There had been some luridly crossed wires, and that never helps.

We approached the warehouse windows together, after the explanations. The man was Detective Sergeant MacCarthy. He'd happened to be in Carlisle, working with the local police on a discovery of an arms dump in a seedy terrace house in the town, when instructions had come through from Belfast. He was to go to Glasgow in connection with the warehouse and take a look around. He'd checked in with Glasgow police and that duty inspector had never told me. Maybe nobody had told *him*. I asked, why the orders from Belfast?

He said, "Your people in Focal House. They'd contacted Defence Ministry."

"I knew that," I said. "So?"

"Defence Ministry contacted us. There was talk of a possible IRA involvement. We always react to that."

"Of course. It's just that no-one informed me, that's all. As you said – a cock-up. And you acted like a tail," I added bitterly. MacCarthy apologised; I saw it plain now. Two of us with the single thought, to take a private look. MacCarthy, with years of RUC experience behind him, didn't trust the mainland police to do the sort of job he was himself accustomed to do when dealing with suspected IRA activities. He and his RUC colleagues knew the IRA a sight better than anyone in the rest of Britain. I asked him what he thought about the likelihood of the IRA being involved this time.

"I'd not be surprised," he said, "not surprised at all."

"No hard evidence?"

"No."

"Do you see a threat developing to Stirling Castle?"

"Stirling Castle?" That had surprised him. "Why should that be?"

I said, "Just an idea. You'll be aware that the Libyan terrorist's been moved to Stirling, of course. Al Kufra – and his friends out to secure his release."

"I know that," he said. "But just because of that, Stirling's not a soft target exactly – "

"The IRA don't always go just for the soft targets, do they?"

"Well, no, they don't." MacCarthy admitted. We exchanged theories, briefly. MacCarthy agreed with my notion that the IRA wouldn't be giving two pins if Al Kufra got blown to oblivion; terrorists were not always mates and the IRA cared about no-one but themselves and their aims. He agreed with Max's view, that Stirling Castle would be a very prestigious target but he also said that there had been no suggestion from Belfast that anyone was after it. He believed it was something of a red herring. I didn't go on to tell him about the apparent resurgence of Tokushima. That, for now, was under wraps and I didn't want to cross any wires with Max and his dealings with Whitehall.

So we went through the window. MacCarthy managed that without needing to break it. He climbed up onto the sill, with great agility for a heavily-built man, and inserted some instrument into the side of the frame and wrenched it open. We dropped down into thick darkness, into a small space between the wall and the hides. We kept still for around two minutes, just listening.

No sound at all. A dead stillness that could almost be felt. I switched on my torch. In its beam I saw the close stacks of animal hides, just as I had left them with Felicity the night before.

I said, "We'd better find the hatch, Sergeant. The one I was taken down." He knew all about that; Belfast had filled him in after getting that alert from Defence Ministry. We found the main alley between the hide stacks, and turned to the left at the end. It took me some while and a lot of useless heaving of the stock before I found the hatch. I got down on my stomach and felt around for the light switch, and turned it on.

I led the way down the ladder into the now brightly-lit concrete passage. We looked in through the glazed slits of the doors. The crates were there still, looking intact though I assumed the police would have opened each of them. They'd made a neat job of replacing the lids. MacCarthy tried one of the doors and it opened, and we went in.

We lifted the lids again, MacCarthy using a small jemmy. They were all empty as the police had reported. We went through all the other storerooms: all empty.

"Well now," MacCarthy said. "It looks like an arms dump, that's certain."

"But no arms."

"I'd not be too certain about that, Commander."

"No?"

"No. There could be another stowage."

"But they'd have had time to remove the lot." I was remembering that sojourn in the tenements; they'd had all night before I'd been able to alert the police.

"That may be so," MacCarthy said. "But by all accounts, that's to say according to Glasgow police, the villains went to a deal of trouble to obtain legal possession of this warehouse. To me, that speaks of a big dump, a very big dump indeed. Sure they may have removed some of it, the easily found part. But the IRA don't give up easy, you see. They hang on to their dumps, if you follow me. And there's maybe somewhere it's not going to be found easily."

"We'd better start on it," I said, but MacCarthy disagreed.

"Ah no," he said. "Why put ourselves to the bother of that? They'll be back for it, you see."

"With the police – "

"Never mind the police, Commander. The word'll be back with the villains that the police have made their search and found nothing and that the premises are not under surveillance. For my money, they'll not be long."

I grunted; I was amazed that there had been no surveillance and I said as much. MacCarthy had the answer to that as well. He said, "Wheels within wheels, Commander. The place isn't entirely without surveillance. We're here, are we not, just as soon as we reasonably could be? Though we didn't expect to find each other."

So that was it: I read between the words. MacCarthy had got the RUC in Belfast to play it his way. Call off the Glasgow police and do it himself. It explained quite a lot, one way and another. Except one thing. I asked, "How come the IRA will fall for it, not smell a rat?"

He answered that with another question. "Have you yourself ever come up against the IRA before, Commander?"

I said I had not. He gave a chuckle. "I thought not. The IRA in my experience . . . let me put it this way, Commander. You'll have heard of some of the cock-ups they've made in the past. Blowing up themselves instead of the intended victim. Blowing up the wrong victim because they'd mis-timed or been misinformed. And you'll have heard the jokes about dim Irishmen. They're not all as daft as they seem – *they happen.* Although I say it meself . . . it's the Irish in us! You'll see, Commander."

So we waited; waited, back in the dark soon after, for an Irish cock-up. MacCarthy was convinced it wouldn't be the kidnappers themselves who would show. It would, he said, be someone from the IRA come to take over the shipment. He believed also that whoever came would very likely be known to him. That was another little bit of explanation in its way: MacCarthy was here to cross a few Ts from Belfast. It was all getting very involved.

We had shifted from the cellar regions, back to the main warehouse. We waited in cover, a little way up one of the clear spaces between the hide stacks. The grimy windows showed no light; it was still some way to the dawn. I reckoned that if anyone came it had to be by night. They would scarcely risk it in daylight. Not even the Irish . . . MacCarthy knew his own countrymen but I thought he was being a little over-confident. I could be wasting my time; the IRA was not my main concern, far from it – I wasn't here to assist MacCarthy make arrests of his own. Yet there was that link, and if we bowled out the IRA we might at the same time bowl out the Friends of Al Kufra and save a lot of nastiness around Stirling Castle. I wouldn't like to see anything happen there; the castle had a proud history and looked magnificent set upon its high rock that overlooked the field of Bannockburn where in 1314 Robert the Bruce had defeated the English under Edward II. Once, I'd been taken over the castle as a guest of the regimental secretary of the Argyll and Sutherland Highlanders. The regimental secretary, Colonel Anderson, was also the curator of the museum. He had taken an obvious pride in that museum and in his regiment's long and distinguished record from Wellington's campaigns to Aden in the 1960s. The museum was full of valuable silver, great centre-pieces for mess tables, smaller things such as an ornate snuffbox that had been given to the regiment by the last of its officers to survive Corunna, all of them with their individual and personal stories, like the cases of medals won in battle, many of them VCs. In the Mess, oil paintings of former Colonels of the Regiment filled the walls; a comfortable ante-room contained big leather armchairs and old, well-polished furniture. A stairway led up and out to the battlements with a fine view over where Bruce had achieved that resounding victory for his Scots.

If anything should happen there because of Al Kufra, or to satisfy the IRA's presumptuous pride, a great slice of Scottish history would be gone forever. The castle was strongly founded and had been built of massive stone and it had weathered the centuries to stand as strongly as ever. But it had never yet had to withstand modern high explosive, and I

91

was well aware of what the IRA had done in the past by way of massive explosions. Those high battlements immediately above the priceless regimental silver in the museum and Mess would surely crumble when the supports below were blown away.

In a low voice I spoke of this to Detective Sergeant MacCarthy. He said, "Well, yes, it's likely enough. But it's inanimate just the same. Not like the people who'll be killed. Or the hundreds who've already been killed, in Northern Ireland and elsewhere. It's them I think about. The human tragedies – you know what I mean. And all for a dream. A dream of a united Ireland that will never be."

"You think not?"

"I *know* not. Unite Ireland by some agreement between governments, and still you have the Irish people themselves, the Protestants and the Catholics. Neither side will ever stop fighting the other, whatever the governments have to say about it."

I didn't ask Detective Sergeant MacCarthy which religion he followed; there were Catholics in the RUC, Catholics loyal as Protestants to the British crown, which added, really, to the enigma that was Ireland. So many Catholics from Eire had fought with the British in the war, though they had no compulsion so to do, coming as they did from a neutral country. The boyos of the IRA were not basic Ireland. They took their ideas and their arms from outside. Like now. Their allies were all men engaged in world terrorism. Again, like now. Like the Friends of Al Kufra, and the men we had fought against in Operation Tokushima, men like Kyoshiro Ka. Unthinking terrorism for its own sake, master-minded by fanatics without mercy, without humanity, who would stop at nothing.

I wondered if Max was getting anywhere with the Whitehall mandarins. I wondered what Brian Horley would achieve in Teheran, whether he would vanish to become yet another hostage in the cauldron of the Middle East.

Dawn came and nothing had happened. It was deadly cold in that warehouse. We didn't move much; we had to make no sound that might be picked up. I was weary and hungry and thirsty. I began to think we were wasting our time but MacCarthy had the patience of absolute certainty. In time, he said, someone would be sure to come. "It stands to reason," he said, but didn't elaborate further on reason.

We went on waiting as the light crept up behind the grime of the windows.

"There now," MacCarthy said in a whisper, laying a big hand on my arm. "D'you hear it?"

I did. A vague sound, very faint. It was hard to pin-point the direction but it seemed to me to be coming from where I would least have expected it – from below, from the cellar where Felicity and I had been held.

We listened intently.

MacCarthy whispered, "I don't believe it's in the cellar exactly, Commander. I don't believe that at all. But it's close enough to the cellar to make it sound that way."

"A penetration from outside – a tunnel?"

"Something of that sort, I believe. I suggest we go down. Without putting on the light this time."

I agreed. Taking it very carefully, on tiptoe, we made our way back to the hatch, once again covered with the camouflaging animal hides. This time I found the spot without difficulty, and, again with immense care, we shifted the hides and opened up the hatch. No light, but we had our torches ready for use when necessary.

I felt for the treads with my feet and we went down. Now the sounds were louder, and grew louder still as we went along the concrete-lined passage. A sound like dragging, something heavy. A thump, as though something had impacted against a wall. No sound of voices.

We went along fast. We reached the end of the corridor and found nothing. Just that strange sound, continuing to our right. MacCarthy whispered in my ear, "One thing's sure. There's another cellar, with another entry. A cellar contiguous with this one. And now I guess it's being emptied. We'll be doing no good down here, I'm thinking, Commander."

"Back up again, then," I said.

93

"That's it. Then go outside and take them by surprise."

So we went back, using the torches now and taking it much faster. I left the hatch closed but uncovered, and we moved fast through the warehouse, now in murky daylight. When we reached the window, squeezing between the stacks and the wall, MacCarthy climbed up to look through. Jumping down again, he said, "There's no-one there, the yard's deserted. No vehicle, no men."

"Outside – beyond the perimeter wall?"

He nodded. "It has to be, hasn't it? The tunnel you spoke of, Commander. A manhole beyond the wall. And I'm thinking there'll be a lorry waiting on the cleared ground, where it'd not look unduly suspicious to anyone passing by." He paused. "I think we'll just take a look now."

Once again he climbed to the window, opened it, and dropped to the ground. I reached up to climb myself. As I came level with the window I saw a man pull himself to the top of the wall from the outside. I yelled a warning. MacCarthy saw him, and saw the revolver in the hand. Going again into reflex action, he fired. But the man on the wall was faster. The bullet took Detective Sergeant MacCarthy in the chest and he went down gurgling blood.

9

I got the man who had killed MacCarthy. My first shot blew
him from the wall. He wasn't dead, or anyway not right away.
I heard the screaming and a pain-racked supplication to the
Holy Mother of Jesus. I jumped down from the window, into
the yard, and ran for the locked gates. There was no more
firing but I heard a vehicle starting up beyond the perimeter
wall. As fast as I could I climbed over the gates and ran round
the street wall of the warehouse, making for the corner where
the road led past the tenements. A big closed van was belting
along the road, too far off already for me to read the number
plate. I went onto the cleared ground where it had presumably been waiting. There was blood dripping down the wall
but there was no body.

I found the manhole hypothesised by Detective Sergeant
MacCarthy. I didn't see it at first; not until I'd seen the
hastily scuffed earth, the attempt at a fast and rather useless
concealment. Beneath this, set around six inches below the
earth, was a large square iron hatch. I tugged at a ring sunk
into the metal and with an effort lifted it a little way. Then I
let it go back. The villains were not likely to return again,
though they might well have been interrupted in their work. I
could leave the final clearance to the police. My first priority
now was to alert the nick and then contact Max. I ran along
towards the tenement building and found the p.c. on guard.
He had seen no lorry going past; he'd been checking round the
back. He asked had it left me behind, or what?

I told him who I was. He was not the constable of the night
before and after I'd given my name he remembered he'd seen

me around the station. I asked him to call up police HQ on his transceiver and he went into action commendably fast, passing my message and asking for a search party.

"And a car to pick me up," I said.

"Take you to the station, sir?"

"Yes," I said. I wasn't going to wait for the police search of the new cellar. Either they would find arms or they wouldn't; I would be informed quickly enough. The police car was with me within fifteen minutes and inside another fifteen I was talking to Focal House on the security line. The duty officer: Max wasn't available. I passed the word that an officer of the RUC had been killed and that in my view an IRA involvement could now be considered certain. I'd heard that Irish voice and the Catholic invocation. Max, the duty officer said, would be in touch as soon as possible.

I rang off and checked the time: a little after eight-thirty. The hospital consultant wouldn't have made his rounds yet and Felicity would still be a patient. I called the hospital and spoke to the ward; the sister said Miss Mandrake was fine and would probably be discharged about noon. I knew the police guard was still there outside her cubicle and I'd already arranged that she would be collected by a car from the nick. No worries there.

Before Max rang back word had come in from the police at the warehouse: a tunnel had indeed led from the manhole outside the perimeter wall and at the end of it they'd found that other cellar as suggested by MacCarthy. They didn't think it was anything new, nothing built recently for the purpose of stashing arms and explosives. The walls were old brick and were crumbling in places. Undoubtedly arms and explosives had been there, however; some were there still, but not a lot. Some cases of small-arms ammunition, one of grenades, an AK-47 assault rifle. What was much more alarming was that there were some spares, and those spares were for SAM-7 anti-aircraft missiles and for some highly sophisticated electronics stuff for interfering with the security forces' attempts to pick up radio-controlled bombs. There were also traces of a wickedly powerful Czechoslovakian plastic explosive – Semtex. Something very nasty that would mean much trouble for whatever the target was to be.

I still saw that target as Stirling Castle.

I said so to Max. As before, he didn't disagree. He confirmed that he'd passed the word to Defence Ministry and thence, as of course I knew already, to the Royal Ulster Constabulary. He also agreed now with an IRA involvement.

I asked, "What about Teheran?"

"Horley's on his way."

"With Whitehall's approval?"

There was a short laugh. "What Whitehall doesn't know about – you know the rest, Shaw. Spatchcock's leaving it to us. You know that too. What are you going to do now?"

I asked if he had any specific orders. He said he had not. Spatchcock was leaving it to Max; and Max was leaving it to me. I saw myself as a sort of pig in the middle. Then I said I was going to Belfast. There, I said, I would try to get to the heart of the matter before anything happened in Stirling. Security, Max said, was being heavily stepped up and he didn't believe anything or anybody would get through. In my mind I heard what would have been the comment of MacCarthy if he'd been alive: that the IRA could find ways of getting through anything. After every outrage, MacCarthy would probably have said, military security had been stepped up but still the IRA had always found its target.

Max asked, "Do you propose to take Miss Mandrake to Belfast?"

"No," I said. "I'm not risking her, not after what's happened."

"I think that's wise," he said. He, no more than I, had any wish to risk another hostage-taking exercise. He passed orders for Felicity: she was to leave Glasgow by air under police escort and would be picked up by our people at Heathrow whence she would be helicoptered direct to the pad on the roof of Focal House. Max then cut the call and I was driven to the hospital for a word with Felicity, in advance of the consultant's rounds. She was cheerful, really for my sake, I thought, but she couldn't conceal her anxiety about my going across to

97

Northern Ireland. When I left her, I saw the sparkle of tears. I believe she didn't expect to see me again. The IRA were playing for very high stakes.

I went across by air as an ordinary fare-paying passenger, dressed by courtesy of the nick's CID in casual clothes – faded jeans, T-shirt and anorak, heavy boots white in colour. The anorak was good cover for my shoulder holster: and advance word had gone across to Aldergrove that a Mr Brown would by police authority be carrying a gun and he was to be passed through without comment.

At Aldergrove I was met by an unmarked car with a plain clothes driver and taken, not to RUC headquarters but to Stormont, the seat of government. In a big, expensively-furnished room I met a number of well-known faces from the mainland, from the Northern Ireland secretariat and from the Republic, the latter just as anxious as anyone else to see the IRA clobbered and their designs frustrated. I elaborated on the hypothesis propounded in Focal House: that the IRA were in cahoots with the Friends of Al Kufra and also with the Japanese-North Korean consortium who had, as I believed, supplied the arms in Glasgow that were about to be used on the mainland. I also put the point, without at that stage making any mention of a possible allowed escape of Al Kufra, that the jailed terrorist might perhaps be used in negotiations with Teheran on certain British interests.

"What would these interests be?" the man from Dublin asked.

I said, "That's not my concern. I can't comment. I'm sorry."

"For no comment," the Dublin man observed sardonically, "read oil."

"Maybe," I said, and shrugged.

I was questioned closely about the recent events on the mainland. One of my interviewers was a high-ranking officer of the RUC. I told them about the Bradford coffin shop, the presence of a North Korean national in the farmhouse on the lonely northern fells, the drive in the van and the Glasgow warehouse and its contents, and about the shooting of Detective Sergeant MacCarthy. After around half an hour the man from Dublin left; he had an urgent appointment south of the border, he said. Before leaving he promised full co-operation from his government and from the Garda. He spoke of troubles ahead for Eire, economic difficulties that if things went badly wrong could break up the social order of the Republic. He wanted no IRA ready to step into a power vacuum, nor did his Prime Minister. Except from their own ilk, the IRA would find no support south of the border.

When the Dublin man had gone the Northern Ireland bigwig – who was not the Secretary of State himself – remarked that Al Kufra seemed to have faded into the background.

"Not so," I said. "It revolves around him still." Then I asked, casually, if he knew of a Mr Spatchcock in Whitehall. He did.

"The Spatchcock plan?" he asked, lifting an eyebrow.

Then I knew he knew. I said, "Right."

"Sounds pretty hare-brained," he said, "but then so is Spatchcock. That's just between these four walls, Commander, of course." He leaned back in his chair and studied the high, ornate ceiling for a moment or two. "Certainly Teheran might play ball. They like intrigue, always have, and I suppose there *is* much to be gained. But if anything should ever leak . . . that's the danger." His eyes came back from aloft. "Do we know the timing?"

"Of the escape? *I* don't," I said. "And I don't imagine anyone else does at this stage. It depends, as I gather, on what our man – 6D2 – achieves in Teheran."

"Or doesn't achieve."

"One of the imponderables at this moment," I said. Then I asked, "Has anyone considered the further removal of Al Kufra, I wonder? If that was done, the heat would be off Stirling Castle . . . or would it?" Not necessarily, I thought. And the Friends of Al Kufra might well fall out with the IRA if the latter went ahead with their own plans to blow Stirling Castle and in so doing cocked a snook at anything to do with

Al Kufra himself. Really it was all imponderables; but I remembered what Max had said about the need to preserve Al Kufra for that hypothetical assisted escape at least until Brian Horley had had his chance in Teheran. All things being considered a split in the ranks could be a very good thing; and one way of achieving that might be, after all, to shift Al Kufra yet again.

I put the point and it was taken up by the man from Whitehall, who'd gone for a pee just before I'd made my reference to Spatchcock. He was a senior civil servant from the Cabinet Office and he was very cautious. Everything, he said, would be considered, naturally. But I wasn't to forget that moves could be extremely dangerous. "Road convoys . . . you yourself have come up against a plan to attack the convoy taking the prisoner to Stirling. That could so easily have come off, as you must be aware, Commander."

"I'm aware," I said. The talk went on, much of it in my view waffle. There were, as ever, so many yard-arms to be protected, reputations kept unchallenged. It was always un-wise to be too forthcoming. Like Spatchcock. You were best off shifting the responsibility onto someone else, who could then shift it further.

I was glad I'd never been drawn to the civil service, or even parliament. I was growing restive under question and answer and to bring it to an end I said I would appreciate a full run-down on recent IRA activities in the Province. This was seen as reasonable and once again I was given an unmarked car with driver and was taken to RUC headquarters.

There were large-scale maps, charts showing the location of the various outrages that almost always, though often directed at purely military targets, seemed to include innocent civilian casualties. Bystanders, women and children among them, caught in the wicked explosions that came more and more frequently without any advance warning. Once, the IRA had given those warnings by telephone. Now they had grown more cold-blooded. But the unofficial, illegal Protestant backlash was often just as cold-blooded. It was an eye for an eye

100

situation when the Protestant extremists went into retaliation. There seemed to be no hope of an end to it all. Even the Roman Catholic church hierarchy was cutting no ice, any more than the Church of Ireland. Cardinals and Bishops fulminated, pleading in anguish from the pulpit, but all ears were deaf and the slaughter went on. Ambushes in the country districts. Off-duty RUC men and members of the Ulster Defence Regiment, killed in front of their families. Serving English infantrymen, trying to keep the peace impartially, brutally done to death with the mobs baying their approval. I had known all this, of course; but to hear it at first hand from police officers who had suffered it, in some cases, for all their careers, brought it home vividly and poignantly. All, as dead MacCarthy had said in Glasgow, for a wildly impossible dream, a dream fostered by wicked men. I marvelled that Belfast should look so normal on the surface. During the two drives that day I'd seen men and women carrying on as usual as though all was fine, but no doubt knowing all the time that a bomb could detonate at any moment or a man could be seized when helping his wife with the shopping, seized by hooded men and shot in full view of all, and the hooded men would walk away with impunity.

Still in the name of Brown I booked as recommended by the police superintendent into a hotel in the city centre of Belfast after leaving RUC HQ. I pondered on Al Kufra; I thought once again about the advisability of shifting him from Stirling. Of course, there was that risk of attack whilst on the road. That was real enough; and I had to assume that the villains would get to know of any move in time to set up such an attack. Their intelligence would be good, possibly even derived from within the prison services itself. So perhaps the risk really was too great.

I had checked into my hotel room only around twenty minutes when my telephone burred. The caller said, "RUC, Mr Brown. You're wanted on the phone by London. Security line. There's urgency, we gather. We're sending a car – it'll be with you in ten minutes. Is that okay, Mr Brown?"

"It'll have to be," I said, and rang off. Then I called back, as a safety check. When the call was confirmed as genuine I went down to the reception area and waited, wondering what Max had to impart – it would probably have been Max calling, I thought. Sharp on the ten minutes a man came in from the street and started looking about and I approached him. A plain clothes man, one I'd not seen before.

"Name of Brown?" he asked.

I said that was me, and he produced his identity card. I went out with him to the car, an unmarked one as before. I saw two other men sitting in the car, one in front in the driving seat, another in the back. I'd made that check call so it ought to be all right but the presence of other men told me it wasn't all right at all. I stopped short of the car and said, "Just a minute."

"What's the matter, Mr Brown?"

"This," I said, and brought out the automatic from my shoulder holster. The man with me on the pavement reacted fast, shooting from his pocket but missing me. I fired back and got him between the eyes. He went down and the car moved off, the man in the back firing through the wound-down window. His bullets found two civilians, an elderly woman and a youth. Someone in the hotel was fast; within three or four minutes an ambulance was speeding in, and then a police car. I asked if they were the crew sent to pick me up. They were not; but they said they'd had word on their radio that just eight minutes earlier an unmarked police car had been shot up at traffic lights in Victoria Street and the driver killed. That could have been my car. The IRA could no doubt home in on the police frequency and get all the facts they needed to substitute a pickup of their own.

"That's Belfast," the police driver said. The man on whom I'd pulled my gun was dead according to the ambulance crew. He would be identified later, the RUC driver said.

Since the original call to my hotel room had been genuine, I was driven to HQ to see what Max had to say. When my call went through to him, I reported first of all that I appeared already to have been rumbled by the IRA. He didn't like that but didn't seem much surprised. He told me he had further

102

news about Al Kufra: Brian Horley had gone into action immediately on arrival in Teheran, no time wasted, and the Teheran authorities appeared willing to play along the Spatchcock lines.

I asked, "Does this mean the assisted escape?"

"Not so fast," Max said. "There's time yet – "

"But the Friends of Al Kufra – "

"They'll be given certain orders from Teheran if it comes to that, Shaw. Orders to hold off."

"That won't necessarily apply to the IRA if Stirling Castle's their target," I said.

Max agreed. The IRA was now the chief anxiety. The heat was off Al Kufra, just a little, and maybe only for just a while depending on Brian Horley. Max went on to say that a shift was being considered, just to throw a spanner into the IRA's works. A move to Carlisle Castle, but so far no decisions had been taken. I asked, "Is this part of the Spatchcock plan too?"

Max said it might be; he was cautious, non-committal; but we both knew what we were talking about: the assisted escape that might yet be on the cards. A faked-up attack on the road convoy from Glasgow to Carlisle, during which Al Kufra might be allowed to scarper? If murder was Belfast, I thought, deviousness was undoubtedly London. Thinking this, I missed the next utterance from Max. I asked for a repeat. Irritably, he said, "Safi Suduteh, alias Behzad Habibi."

"What about him?"

"He's been picked up by the Bradford police. Do you want to talk to him?"

I said I did; he was very valuable and might cough up gold. I would go at once to Bradford where Safi Suduteh was being held and then return to Belfast, unless events subsequent to the interrogation sent me elsewhere. Before I rang off I asked Max about Felicity.

"Miss Mandrake's remaining in Focal House," he said, and didn't elaborate. He cut the call. I knew the score, of course. Virtual imprisonment, for her own safety's sake. She wouldn't be liking that but I was much relieved.

The RUC was nicely free with its transport: I was once again given a car back to the hotel so that I could pack my grip and check with reception that the room would be held for me. I left cash from my expense account to cover a full week. In point of fact I would not return to the hotel. I would find another and hope to keep one jump ahead of the IRA that way – they already knew I'd checked into this hotel so henceforward it would be unsafe for use, but it wouldn't do any harm for them to get to hear I'd reserved the room.

All this done, I went up in the lift to my room. I used my key and had just got inside when everything went black; I was conscious of a violent blow on the side of my head, that was all. The rest emerged later, when I sat dizzily in a car being driven rapidly out of Belfast.

10

I was aware of passing through mean streets, past dereliction
and hoardings covered with IRA slogans and other graffiti;
but I didn't know Belfast so I didn't pick up the direction. In
any case I was feeling like death, with a blinding headache
that throbbed like a drum. But when we came to a motorway I
saw the signs for Londonderry. The men in the car didn't
speak and I wasn't physically ready to ask questions. I could
assess for myself how I'd been ambushed and how I'd been
spirited out of the hotel afterwards: I'd noted a service lift near
my room, and there could have been collusion from the hotel
staff. In Northern Ireland you didn't really know in many
cases who was your friend.

Londonderry, or just Derry as the Republicans called it,
disliking any suggestion of England: the place where the
Apprentice Boys held their annual march in commemoration
of that event in December 1688 when their youthful forbears
had shut the gates of the town against the Catholic garrison;
and then eighteen months later William of Orange had beaten
King James II at the Battle of the Boyne and soon after that
the Loyal Orange Institution was formed, thus perpetuating
the long war between the Protestant and Catholic communi-
ties. So much I knew from my school history books; and had
learned much since, when each year those modern-day
counterparts of the original Apprentice Boys paraded with
their pipe bands wearing the provocative saffron kilt.

I knew, too, about the Creggan and the Bogside, those no-
go areas under the domination of the IRA gunmen. The lairs
from which the bombings were planned. I remembered what

had happened at Ballykelly around seven years earlier.

We'd be going to the Creggan or the Bogside, I thought. Once in Londonderry we passed the normal shopping crowds, some of whom would be British servicemen from the infantry battalion stationed in the city with their support units. No uniforms: they were too dangerous. On the surface of it all I was in the midst of normality. But the gun pressed against my side was the unspoken warning not to start anything that would attract attention.

It was one of the no-go areas all right: the atmosphere was at once different. A feeling of unease, of watchful eyes in sullen faces, more hoardings after we'd been let through the road blocks, more graffiti, all of it in support of the IRA. Brits Out. Death to the Murderers. In places some faded exhortations: Death to Thatcher, with other and cruder references. The men in the car seemed to be known: it was almost a home-coming. Men and women waved from the streets and were answered, grim-faced, by a flick of the hand.

The car drove into what looked like a builder's yard, where it stopped. Wooden gates were shut behind it by a man who'd come out of a shack in the yard.

I was told to get out, which, in front of the guns, I did. I was pushed in through the back door of a house to one side of the yard. I was pushed into a room, a biggish room with a long table round which men sat as though at a board meeting. Some of them well-dressed like professional men who could easily have been such – doctors, architects, bank managers, accountants. Others not. All wore black hoods. There was one at the head of the table, four at each side. An empty chair stood at the table's foot, and I was told to take it.

My head ached more than ever; my mouth was dry as dust – seemed filled with dust. I felt the caked blood down the back of my head and neck, and my shoulders were stiff.

I asked for water.

The man at the head of the table said, "Bring him water."

One of the men from the car left the room and I heard a tap running. He came back in with a glass. I drained it. The man

106

who seemed to be the chairman, a heavy man and tall with it, very big indeed, said, "First your report."

The man who had brought the glass gave it. "No trouble," he said. "Not after the effort that aborted, that is."

The black hood dipped in a nod. "Yes. That's been seen to. Orders have gone to Belfast . . . Patrick and Kevin, they've already been knee-capped. It'll not happen again."

Yes, I thought, it had been foolish of them to have that pickup car manned with extras, a dead giveaway. I recalled what Detective Sergeant MacCarthy had said about his own race, the liability to stupid cock-ups that were so often a decided asset to the security forces.

After that the questioning started. I had nothing to tell them. They knew Al Kufra was in Stirling Castle; they knew as much as I did, apart from the fact that he was likely to be moved to Carlisle, about which I said nothing. I got the impression, which as it happened confirmed my own earlier reflections, that they were not particularly interested in Al Kufra himself. They were not very convinced allies of the Friends of Al Kufra. What they wanted to find out from me was how much was known to the security forces about their own involvement.

I asked, sitting there with the guns close, "Involvement in what?"

"Don't act the innocent," the big man said. "You're not grass green. Why has 6D2 come in on this?"

I shrugged. "Because of Al Kufra."

"That's all?"

"That's all," I said.

"A likely one is that! What about Glasgow, and the man MacCarthy?"

I said, "You had him killed. That's what about him. I don't know about anything else."

"You were there with him, for God's sake!"

"Sheerly fortuitous," I said. "Part of the operation to preserve Al Kufra."

"Preserve?"

"Keep him where he belongs. In jail."

"Ach, that's you Brits all over! The man's a freedom fighter."

I said, "Well, I suppose that's how you would regard him. You're freedom fighters too, aren't you?"

"Yes."

"Guns, bombs, murders. All done in a cowardly way. Freedom? Language today has taken a funny turn."

"You'll not be finding it funny for much longer," the big man said, and he was right. It was very far from funny and it left me in no condition even to think straight. Before it started, before I was taken to another room, the big man told me what I knew already: that I would find no friends in the Creggan. There would be no RUC here, no military, to get me out. Not ever again. I could simply disappear and no-one beyond the Creggan or the Bogside would know where or how I'd died. Not even a body would be found. This I knew to be nothing but the truth: they had done it before, many times. The security forces liked to think that they had the gunmen on the run, that they were winning slowly but surely – but this I doubted. Certainly they had made their arrests, but never enough. For each terrorist caught, ten or twenty more were not. And always there were new ones coming along, the boys that became youths and then men after a lifetime spent in the surroundings and trappings of terrorism, brought up with their mothers' milk to believe in the bravery and idealism of the IRA, in their version of freedom, of Ireland for the Irish. It was in their blood, firmly and for ever. The IRA had bred and was still breeding terrorists for their political use.

So the unfunny part began.

It lasted a long time. Or I think it did. It seemed to, anyway. Not much imagination, not much finesse. The men who were turned loose on me were simply thugs. One of the black hoods was put over my head and tied. I was hit by fists, pummelled from one to another till I fell with dizziness. Heaved up again, the beating went on. Clubs were used next, all over my body. Shoes and socks were removed and I was held down while cigarette butts were burned into the soles of my feet. Something, a razor blade I believe, cut the flesh

108

between my toes. The pain was agonising. When I was made to stand up again, the floor was slippery with blood. I was kicked and kneed where it hurt most.

I didn't say anything. Not a word. I tried to concentrate my thoughts away from what was happening, tried to think of Max in Focal House, even of Spatchcock safe and wily in the cosiness of the Whitehall ambience, of Felicity thankfully immured in Focal House and away from nastiness. I tried to think of past days and nights spent in her company. The better times; but it didn't really work out. The present was much too real for make-believe.

In the end I passed out.

I hadn't said anything at all. When I passed out, I suppose they gave up, anyway for the time being. When I came to I was in pain all over and again very thirsty. My lips, my whole face, felt like pulp. I was lying on something soft, not a bed. I saw later that it was a sofa. Curtains were drawn across a window and there was daylight seeping through. I don't know how long I'd been out; possibly all or most of the night. It was painful to open my eyes even in that dim light, green from the curtain's colour, and I closed them again. From somewhere outside the room, I heard a voice singing, not untunefully.

"Oh, Paddy dear, and did ye hear
The news that's goin' round?
The shamrock is be law forbid
To grow on Irish ground . . ."

"That's Seamus," a voice behind me said, a girl's voice. I'd not been aware of anyone else in the room with me; she had kept very quiet and still. She spoke again. "I saw you were lookin' around yourself. How're you feelin'?"

I didn't answer that. I said, "I assume you've got a gun."

"Sure I have. And Seamus too." Like the others, the accent was of the south. It was an attractive accent, so was the voice itself. "We'll not be usin' them if you don't give cause. Here's Seamus comin' now," she added as the singing stopped and the door opened. I turned my head a little, eyes open again now, and saw Seamus. He was a youth, no more – about eighteen, a different type of Irishman from the others, who were darkish, long-faced with the long upper lip of some of the Irish. Seamus was of the other sort, merry-faced, blond, with a round, rather chubby face and an open look about him. He looked down at me as he shut the door behind him. "So he's come round," he said to the girl.

"Yes," she said.

"He looks in a bad way, Deidre."

"He is that," she said. "I'll clean him up a little. Is that all right, Seamus?"

"Sure, it's all right," the youth said carelessly. "We're not wanting him to die, are we?" No, I thought, they wouldn't want that; not yet. There would be further questioning first and then I might die. No information extracted – I'd be no use to them when they failed. These weren't the Friends of Al Kufra – they wouldn't need a hostage. The girl came round from behind me and in that dim green light I saw her for the first time. She was tall with a good figure, dressed to show it off, and she had long dark hair, the ends curling round her chin. She was very pretty in that special Irish way. I reckoned she was around twenty or twenty-one and despite the difference in colouring there was a look about her that said she could be Seamus' sister.

She looked down at me with a smile. "God, but you're a mess," she said, and went out. Seamus stayed on guard, an automatic ready in his hand. I shifted on the sofa and felt the tug of ropes around my body; they were taking few chances, not even in the state I was in physically, but my wrists had not been tied. Seamus began humming, another Irish song, this time a revolutionary one. I picked up the refrain of 'The Belfast Brigade':

> "Come all you gallant Irishmen,
> And join the IRA,
> And strike a blow for freedom
> When there comes a certain day . . ."

He stopped, and grinned down at me. "A good tune."

"A rabble-rouser." Someone had once said that the devil had all the best tunes; that someone wasn't far wrong. The Irish could always fool themselves with songs of fervour and sentimentality. The girl Deidre came back with an enamel bowl of hot water and a sponge. She sponged my face and when she rinsed out the sponge I could see the blood in the water. She went on with her work and I felt a shade better.

She said, "You're a good looker when you're cleaned up."

"Thank you," I said sardonically.

"You'll not want to be messed up again."

"No," I said.

"And you'll not want to die."

"No again."

"It's a thousand pities," she said, "that you may have to. Why hold out, will you tell me that?" She sounded sadly impatient with English foibles.

I said, "Because I haven't anything to tell anyway. Not that I would."

"The noble hero."

"No," I said. "Just a patriot."

"So are we."

"Have it your own way," I said.

She frowned. "You're all the same, every mother's son of you. Only England's right."

"Same to you," I said. "For England substitute Ireland."

She didn't appear to mind. She said lightly, "Seems you're feeling better."

"I'll survive," I said. That, she told me, was a stupid thing to say, tempting fate. I was forced to take the point. After I'd been cleaned up facially, the girl sent Seamus off to bring some food, first asking me what I'd like. "There's Kellogg's cornflakes," she said. "Bacon and eggs, too."

I said I wasn't hungry; but I knew I had to eat whatever the effort. I settled for dry toast and strong coffee. And a cigarette. All these were brought. I munched the toast down but enjoyed the coffee and cigarette. As I smoked, the girl dragged up a hard upright chair and sat on it, facing me, her expression serious. I saw the swell of her neat breasts, straining the

111

material of the dress. She saw where I was looking and said, "None of that. Don't excite yourself. Tell me about England."

"England?" I was astonished, not expecting this.

"Yes," she said. "Tell me what you Brits think is so bloody special about yourselves that you have to run the whole world."

It was, as I realised, the soft approach now. The rough stuff had failed. Both Seamus and Deidre were friendly apart from the occasional acid remark about the Brits. I didn't tell her much about England; I'm not too good at expressing that sort of thing. In passing I mentioned Mrs Thatcher and the Queen and what they had stood for or still stood for, which was, I said, freedom under the law basically. I spoke of the great English cathedrals and the part religion played in British life, but this was a mistake because she cut in angrily and said all the old cathedrals had been Catholic until Henry VIII had for venal reasons snitched them away; and she spoke of Oliver Cromwell stabling his horses in the Irish churches when he came to Ireland in ruthless conquest. She came, she said, from Galway City, where the Collegiate Church of St James still showed the ring-bolts set in the aisle where the horses had been tethered, but this didn't matter all that much because that particular church was now Church of Ireland, in other words Protestant not Catholic.

I chose the moment to switch from England. I said, "Tell me about Ireland."

"The real Ireland?"

For the second time I said, "Have it your own way."

She told me. She had a long memory, one going back well beyond her own years, based upon tales told by her grandfather about the undoubted atrocities of the Black and Tans back in the early to middle twenties. She didn't mention the ambushes set by the IRA in which so many innocents had died by the bomb and by rifle fire, she didn't mention the Southern Irish Protestants dragged from their beds and put up against walls to be shot out-of-hand so that their land holdings could be seized. I didn't tell her that I'd had an Irish

112

Protestant grandmother myself from whom I'd heard that other side of the sorry Irish story. I didn't think that would be tactful in the circumstances. As she talked she grew more and more Irish, her eyes taking on a stare of concentrated patriotic fervour, her head tossing her hair aside now and again. I let her go on, having no option. She spoke of the small white-washed cottages and the lives of the peasantry who lived in them, of the single room with the turf fire shared by all for sleeping and eating, of the straw palliasses on which the sleeping and the procreation took place while the remnants of the old Protestant Ascendancy lived off the fat of the Irish land once the Troubles had died away for the time being. She spoke of the great beauties of the south and west, of Killarney's lakes, of the mountains of Connemara, the great sweep of Galway Bay towards Aran where the men made their frugal living from the fishing. All that and a lot more; plenty of eloquence. After a while Seamus told her to turn it off and they had a bit of a barney about that and then they began asking the questions again. They gave me another cigarette and asked if I had a girlfriend whom I'd want to see again.

I said no, I hadn't.

Deidre laughed. "Queer, are you?"

I said I wasn't queer and she said, "All right, you needn't bother. We do know about the Mandrake woman after all."

"By courtesy of the Friends of Al Kufra, no doubt."

She nodded. I remarked that that confirmed that they were in cahoots. She said, "We're international."

"Yes," I said, "I know that. North Korea for one – "

"So you do know that much?"

I said, "I saw a Korean when I was in the hands of the Friends. You'll know all about that."

She nodded again. She was very cool and her gun-hand was steady as a rock. "Yes, we know."

"Japanese arms," I said.

"Sure. Why deny it? Not direct from Japan. Fed through Libya and the USA, via Eire."

Of course, there had to be those connections. That was inevitable. NORAID was ever active, dedicated to non-belief in anything the British Government said. And there was Colonel Gaddaffi, the spider in the Libyan web, also dedicated against Britain. I parried further questions and I parried them in such a way that I was able to extract a little information for my own use, if ever it could be put to use. They had become a little careless, seeing it as quite safe, I supposed, since I wasn't going to get away from them ... I took a chance and mentioned a name: I happened to know, I said, that Safi Suduteh had been taken into custody.

"Safi Suduteh?"

"Alias Behzad Habibi," I said.

There was a sudden tension in the atmosphere though they both tried to play it down. They studiously didn't catch each other's eye. Seamus asked, "So what?"

"He'll be talking," I said. "I'd like to be a fly on the wall when he starts."

"It'll not affect us," Seamus said. "Not a little bit at all."

"But you know who he is, don't you?"

"I never said that. I'll make a guess. He's to do with Al Kufra, is he not?"

I laughed. "As if you didn't know!"

Seamus brushed that aside. He said contemptuously, "Al Kufra's of no interest to us. To the IRA – "

"But the Friends of Al Kufra – they believe he is. Isn't that right?"

This time it was Seamus who laughed. "They can believe what they like, it's no skin off our noses. They have their uses, we have ours."

"They want Al Kufra out. You want something else. Like me to make a guess?"

Again Seamus laughed. "Guess away, you bloody Brit, see what good it does you. And it's us that's asking the questions, not you."

After that there was no more exchange of information or guesses. I clammed up and so did they. The soft approach hadn't worked any better than the rough stuff and I braced myself for the next round of beating up, which I fancied wouldn't be long delayed. I believed I'd shaken them by my

114

reference to Safi Suduteh which from the viewpoint of my own physical well-being was probably a mistake. But to rattle them could be nothing but a good thing in the wider context. The girl left the room and when she came back she was accompanied by two of the boyos from the board room. But they hadn't come to beat me up.

I was going for a ride, one of them said. He said it in a melodramatic way; it had the ring of a pre-war American movie. From somewhere in the building I heard the sound of singing, not from Seamus but no doubt from a radio. The 'Londonderry Air' – "and come ye back, When summer's in the meadows . . ."

"That'll not be applying to you," the man said.

The ride didn't in fact start till much later – after dark, when I was taken out into the yard in front of the guns and put into a big car, a Volvo. Seamus and the girl came with me, one on either side in the back, their guns pressing into my sides. The two boyos were in front, one of them driving. We went out from the builder's yard and turned to the left through the traffic, of which there was little enough. We came out from the no-go area and turned over the bridge across the Foyle. The route seemed to be south: we were heading, I supposed, for the Republic and we wouldn't be going through any of the border posts with their customs officials plus the military, the RUC and, on the other side, the Garda. There would be plenty of anonymous ways in; the border wasn't guarded right the way along.

We left the city behind us, coming into open country with the moonlit loom of mountains ahead. We turned off from the main road quite soon, and then turned again onto what was little more than a track, one that petered out in boggy ground. Here the Volvo stopped. I saw a lighted window; and as a man approached from a small cottage behind some heaps of turf laid out to dry, I was told to get out.

"Watch it," one of the gunmen said. "No tricks. This is lonely country."

There was a brief exchange between the men from the car

115

and the newcomer and then the latter turned away. We all followed in single file, coming away from the boggy ground and soon into the cover of the extensive piece of woodland. We went through this, taking it slowly and carefully, and all the men and the girl very watchful. There could, I supposed, be British patrols. If there were, they weren't in our particular vicinity. Coming clear of the trees in a somewhat stony field where cows lay huddled in peaceful sleep, we climbed a stile in a low stone wall and then forded a stream and crossed a railway line.

We came to a small farm. The moon had gone now and there was heavy rain starting. A cart stood in the yard, an old-fashioned affair with a tired-looking horse between the shafts. We all clambered aboard, the guns closing me in. The man who had met us took up the reins.

"Hup, boy," he said to the horse. The animal got into motion. We moved out of the farmyard onto a dusty, rutted road that was turning to mud, again little more than a track. No-one spoke, except for an occasional exhortation from driver to horse. We went for around three miles, as I estimated, and then one of the men from Londonderry at last uttered.

"You are now in the Republic," he said.

I'd never have known it. Nothing marked the border, the land was the same as that of Ulster, as was the man who'd met us the same as the men of the north, as was the man who drove the cart. And we all spoke the same language. It was all so sadly stupid. All the deaths, all the terrorism, all the destruction of property, all in the name of two creeds whose practitioners refused to see sense, refused to find any common ground at all and allowed their very religion to be twisted and bastardised by the guns and bombs of terrorism itself.

11

The rain went on though it lessened in intensity after a while. In the cart, we all became drenched, but there was no let-up in the watchfulness. We went on through the darkness for a few more miles until we reached a country crossroads where Deidre said there had once been *ceilidhs* held on Saturday nights, the only entertainment the Catholic peasantry had had in the old days. She couldn't get away from her obsessions about the Brits and their oppressive ways.

At the cross-roads a car waited. I saw it when the side lights were switched on, presumably when the creak and grind of the cart was heard approaching.

We got into the car, a Ford Granada. Cart and driver turned back the way they had come. The car started off, the seating as before, the guns close. I was dead tired and still sick and sore from the beating-up. I fell asleep. They didn't wake me. I woke of my own accord when the car slowed and I saw the headlights shining on a road sign, a place name. The name was Portsalon. I didn't know anything about Portsalon except that it was on the shore of Lough Swilly, not far south of Fanad Head washed by the North Atlantic, stormed at by the gales of the Western Ocean as seafarers knew it. A longish way from Stirling or Carlisle and right inside the Republic, even though not too far from Londonderry as the crow flies.

The car turned off a little way beyond the sign, making left, away from the small township itself, and again into open country. A long climb began and it ended in another farmyard where the car was driven into a barn and once again I was taken into a house.

117

An old man met us; a very old man with thin white hair and a weather-beaten face. He looked to me not far short of ninety, but even so he was far from decrepit and his voice was strong.

He looked me up and down in the light of a lantern. "So this is the man," he said. "O'Kelly told me about him. What is it you want done?"

"Hold him," one of the Londonderry men said. "You'll be told later what to do with him."

The old man nodded. "And you fellers?"

"Beds for what remains of the night, and breakfast in the morning. Then we'll be on our way." A hint of menace crept into the voice. "And nothing said to a soul. I think you understand, me old Paddywack?"

"There'll be nothing said," the old man answered. "Sure, nobody ever comes here anyway . . ."

The farmhouse was small, little more than an overgrown cottage with whitewashed walls and a roof of thatch. I was taken to a room opening off the main room of the cottage, the sort of place Deidre had spoken of with a turf fire burning in an open hearth and spreading its typical Irish smell and plenty of feather-light ash. In the side room my hands were tied, so were my ankles, and another length of rope ran from under my armpits to a big ring-bolt (shades of Oliver Cromwell and his horses?) set in the wall, which would be strong and durable and probably had been so for the best part of maybe three hundred years. The door into this room, however, was not strong; it was a modern addition that looked totally incongruous, as though it had come from a do-it-yourself supermarket. It didn't keep out sound. Through it I heard talk, a sorting out of the available accommodation for the night. The old man was to banish himself to the straw in the barn where the car was garaged. The two thugs from the Creggan would have the only bedroom, where there was a big bed that had been used by the old man and his wife, now apparently dead. Seamus and Deidre would shake down on the floor of the living room, with straw brought in from the

118

barn. They would be warmed by the remnants of the turf fire.

They were warmed by more than that as it turned out.

They were not, or anyway they shouldn't have been, brother and sister after all. Cousins, maybe. The sounds were easy enough to interpret and the two were very uninhibited about it all. After a while there was silence, apart from heavy breathing. Then I heard them talking. They were talking, I gathered by straining my ears, about the job in hand. The rope tethering me to the ring-bolt had enough slack in it for me to roll a little closer to the door.

I heard Seamus say, "What the Brit was yacking about . . . those daft wet Libyan buggers . . . believing we're worrying our guts out about Al Kufra. The Brits have to be round the twist if that's what they're thinking."

The girl said something that I didn't catch, and then Seamus spoke again. "They'd get nowhere without us and that's a fact. The situation's not changed at all. All those dark faces, Jesus! They'd stand out a mile. The more so to the Jocks."

That was all. If the girl made any further response I didn't hear it. Her voice was too soft, too light. After that the other sounds began again. I kept myself awake as long as I could but there was no further talk between the two of them. I thought about what they had said: dark skins would certainly stand out in Scotland but if mouths were kept shut, it would be hard to differentiate between members of the IRA and the ordinary gawping public. And if as was likely Stirling Castle had been closed to the public for the duration of Al Kufra's stay there, there would be other ways of infiltrating. Tradesmen's vans, men with work to do and work permits to authenticate them, documentation that would be child's play to the forgery sections of the Belfast Brigade. All they had to do was to plant explosives; they weren't going to be there to get Al Kufra out, whatever the Friends might be thinking. Safi Suduteh alias Behzad Habibi was being had for a sucker.

I was convinced now beyond all doubt that Stirling was to be the target. And that would stand whether or not Al Kufra was moved to Carlisle or anywhere else. But one thing

119

remained a mystery. Why did the IRA bother with the Friends of Al Kufra? Why not just go in and set their explosives, and blow Stirling Castle as a prestige gesture? That part didn't quite add up. Surely the job of the IRA would be made more difficult by the security surrounding Al Kufra? Whatever Seamus had to say about it, there had to be some benefit .from the association between the two arms of terrorism.

Morning came. I heard the sounds of breakfast in the main room, then the sound of departure, the car coming out from the barn. Around ten minutes after the Londonderry contingent had gone, the old man came in to me. He brought breakfast with him: a bowl of porridge and a glass of milk. I was ravenous, and thirsty.

I said, "I can't manage with my hands tied."

"I'll be doin' the feedin'," he said, and set down the bowl on the floor, which was bare earth well trampled down over the centuries till it was hard as concrete. He came towards me with the glass and set it to my lips. I brought my head forward and he tilted the glass. I got most of it. Then he brought the bowl and a spoon, and fed me like a baby. Having eaten, I asked for water: the milk hadn't taken away the thirst. He went out and came back with a jug and the drinking process was repeated. I felt a good deal better after that.

I asked, "Where have the others gone?"

"'Tis not your business. Nor mine either."

I didn't suppose he knew: the IRA like to keep the right hand in ignorance of the left whenever possible. I said, "Never mind. I suppose you approve of all the killings . . . all the innocent victims."

"'Tis in a just cause."

"Your church doesn't agree," I said, taking it for granted he was a Catholic.

He said unexpectedly, "Bugger the church." He gave a creaky sort of laugh. "Fall out the RCs," he said. "I'd fallen out long before ivver I heard that order."

"Oh, yes?" I said. "Where did you hear it, then?"

"Before Divine Service. I was once in the British Navy," he

said. I expected him to spit, but he didn't. There had been something in his tone, thinking back . . . I told him I, too, had been in the British Navy.

"Is that a fact?" he asked. "What ships?"

I gave him some names; they were all a long while after his own service and they didn't appear to mean much to him. He said he'd been born in Tipperary and had caught up the tail end of the First World War, serving in what they used to call torpedo-boat destroyers. He spoke nostalgically of those early years; he'd known Pompey well, he said, the roistering of the libertymen from the Royal Naval Barracks in Queen Street and from the warships in the harbour had been great to see and to take part in – the drink and the women. He was a very lapsed Catholic indeed. He'd spent a year at HMS *Vernon*, the torpedo school, qualifying as a diver. As a diver he'd been drafted in 1922 to the old gunboat *Racer*, which was being used as diving ship for the deep-water operation to recover the gold bullion from the White Star liner *Laurentic*, sunk during the war by a German mine at the entrance to Lough Swilly. The *Racer* had been based at Portsalon, and the old man, young then, had married a local girl and had returned there to live when his naval service was over, and he'd worked for his father-in-law, eventually inheriting the small farm.

The old man liked an audience; he led a lonely life, some miles from Portsalon. He seldom visited there these days; the journey was difficult for an old fellow.

He talked about the *Racer*. He'd enjoyed that spell, though it had been hard work, the deepest dive that at that time had ever been attempted. It was away from the main stream of the Fleet. "Not so much of the bull," he said as he looked down at me. "Ah, they were grand fellers, the officers. They treated a man decently."

"So there are some good Brits?"

"There were, yes," he said. "I think many things have gone wrong since. More's the pity."

"The killings?"

"Ach, yes, I think so."

"But you spoke of the cause being just."

121

"That's what they say," he said. "They keep tellin' us that. Even the Holy Joes say that, some of them."

"The priests?"

He nodded. "The parish priests say the killings are just. Not so much the bishops. I take no notice of any of them."

"But you take notice of the IRA?"

"I do," he said. "It's as well to do that." He didn't follow up that remark but the inference was obvious: the old man was under duress but basically he regretted what the IRA had done and was doing. He was not one of the extremists, the terrorists. He went on to talk again about the British Navy, a somewhat rambling discourse about good times and good comradeship in many ships, in many of the world's ports. He spoke of Malta and Gibraltar in the days of Empire, of the great fleets that had lain in Malta's Grand Harbour beneath the shadows of Lascaris and Fort St Angelo; of the nightly beating of retreat by the infantry battalion stationed in Gibraltar. He spoke of fellow Irishmen who had served in the disbanded Irish regiments – Connaught Rangers, Royal Dublin Fusiliers, Leinster Regiment, Munster Regiment . . . his old father had been a corporal in the Connaughts, he said, and he said it with pride.

I asked him what the men from the Creggan meant to do with me. He was very honest. He said, "When they don't want you any more, they'll dispose of you. South from here there are the great bogs. When a man goes into them, he doesn't come out again. And no trace is ever found."

I said, "A kind of deep dive." I felt my flesh creep, just thinking of the sucking mud, the filth, the cutting-off of air.

"A dive," he said, and his voice shook, "that they made my son take. Because they said he was not a patriot. When all he did was to bungle a job in Derry that would have blown up a bus full of children from the British barracks."

"An intentional bungle – is that what you're saying?"

He nodded. "Yes. What would you have done?"

"I hope I'd have done the same," I said. "And you?"

"If I was as brave as my son I would have done the same too. They have gone too far, the wild men. I am too old for it all now." Abruptly he turned away and went back into the main room where the fire was, leaving me to ponder on the all-enclosing bogs of the south.

The old man came back. His lips were trembling and tears were running down his face. Talking to me, talking about days that were gone, had done something to him. We had the shared link of naval service under the crown, and I believe the old chap had a deep feeling for the crown though he had never dared to express it. It had come through in his nostalgic ramblings about the great bases of the old British Empire, in his pride in his father's service, in the many Irishmen who had fought in the British Army against the Kaiser and against Hitler.

Coming back he had a knife in his hand.

He bent and cut the rope holding me to the wall. He cut through the ropes binding my ankles. "Stand up," he said.

I referred to the enormous risk he was taking. As he freed my wrists he said, "Ach, there'll be no risk, none at all. They'll not take me. I have a gun."

"One against many," I said. I tried to thank him, but he waved the thanks away. And he said it wasn't a case of one against many, not at all. The many, he said, would be on his side. "The great majority," he said, and I quite failed to get the reference. "If you take the path away to the north of here it'll take you clear of Portsalon. Down the hillside you come to the lough. By the end of the path there is a boat. As an ex-navy man, you'll find the handling of it easy enough, out past Fanad Head."

Once again I tried to thank him but he wouldn't have it. He went away, back to the main room and the turf fire, while I rubbed the circulation back into my arms and legs until I could move freely. Before I had finished I heard the loud report from beyond that incongruous door; then I knew. I pushed the door open. The old man lay with a sawn-off shotgun that looked as though it had been thrust against his face. The face and part of the head were gone. There was a lot of blood and other matter and a strong stench of gunsmoke.

There was nothing, of course, to be done. Except to make sure the old man's sacrifice wasn't in vain. I left the farm fast and found the track leading to the north. The area was totally deserted. It was a long way and the going was rough; right where he'd said, I found the boat. It was a sailing dinghy, rather the worse for recent neglect, lying on a sandy beach. By superhuman effort I dragged it into the water of Lough Swilly. It floated, with a few leaks that would, or so I hoped, seal themselves when the boat's natural element soaked into the wood. The gear was stiff and rusty with disuse but I got the tatty sail up. There was still no-one around, and it was a clear bright day with enough wind.

As the sail filled, I set a course for Fanad Head, standing clear to the north as I came out from the lee of the land, a small bay that gave shelter from the main stream of the lough. Once outside Lough Swilly I would steer for Malin Head and make through Inishtrahull Sound. Thereafter I could alter towards Glengad Head and Inishowen to enter Londonderry down Lough Foyle: but I would not. The risk was too great. No safety lay there unless I could make immediate contact with the British forces, and that I couldn't guarantee. I would sail the dinghy on for the North Channel for Machrihanish in Kintyre, or maybe up the Firth of Clyde for Greenock, the route home of the wartime convoys of years ago.

12

The weather held; the wind stood fair for the Clyde. With the coast in view I was well able to pick up the landmarks. The distance from Fanad Head to the Tail o' the Bank off Greenock would be around two hundred and fifty miles. It would take a long while, perhaps too long: I had no idea how things were shaping up vis-à-vis Max and Al Kufra, and Brian Horley in Teheran. I didn't fancy trying to make contact with Max from any police station outside Glasgow itself — the security would not be good enough: I couldn't use an outside, unscrambled telephone line. So I wouldn't put into the nearer places such as Ayr or Lamlash.

As it happened I had luck with me still: I was sighted by a helicopter, an RN one out of Machrihanish. I waved, and it came down and hovered and I made contact by old-fashioned semaphore. A man was lowered on the winch and I was gathered up, and the old Irishman's dinghy was left behind as the naval pilot set a course for Glasgow. After touchdown I rang the nick and a car was sent, and I put through my call to Focal House.

"Time's been wasted," Max said. He'd told me to get to London pronto and I'd found him in a foul mood. I refrained from pointing out that it had been a case of *force majeure* and that I was lucky to be there at all. I knew what his response would have been; and he went ahead and made it even though I'd kept silent.

"Shouldn't have damn well allowed yourself to be taken," he said.

"My apologies."

He shifted irritably behind that massive desk. "Tell me what happened, in detail. Then I'll fill you in on what's been happening since you disappeared."

So I told him all about it. I reported what I'd overheard between Seamus and Deidre in between the acts of copulation. I said, "I'm convinced Stirling Castle's the IRA's objective."

"Al Kufra?"

"Not Al Kufra, who could get dented in the blast. Just the castle and as many military personnel as possible." I knew there was no active military presence in the castle, but there were the HQ and museum staff and there were all those items of regimental silver. The Argylls would take their loss very hard indeed. Considerations of security would scarcely allow them to remove it all; the IRA had so far as possible to be kept in ignorance as to how much we knew.

Max said, "They can't be allowed to damage Al Kufra. That's vital."

"Brian Horley?" I asked, and Max nodded. Horley had wasted no time in Teheran. The Iranians, it seemed, were willing to play along the lines of the Spatchcock plan. Certain concessions would be granted if Al Kufra was handed over.

"Or allowed to escape," I said and again Max nodded.

He said, "Those considerations, the concessions by Teheran. They involve a guarantee of continuing supplies of crude oil, which we need to get the right mix with our own North Sea production. Not just that. Contracts for British firms, largely in the construction industry. And a restoration of better relations between our two countries. It all helps to keep out Russian influence. When negotiations are completed, it'll be handed to Whitehall, of course."

Of course. 6D2 could not sign treaties. All the glory would go to Whitehall, if glory there was in a dirty deal, and Spatchcock would in due course figure in an Honours List, a CBE at the very least.

Max was going on. "So, you see, Al Kufra's safety is vital, as I said. Did you glean anything about the time scale, Shaw?"

"The IRA against Stirling Castle?"

"Yes – "

"No," I said. "But I doubt if they'll let any grass grow."

"That's not to be relied upon. They're past masters at lulling the opposition . . . striking when least expected. When the guard's down."

Max was rattled: I'd seldom known him use clichés before. I asked, what about the projected move to Carlisle? He said that was still under consideration. And he confirmed what I'd been thinking whilst in the hands of the Londonderry mob: the shift would provide the opportunity for the escape of Al Kufra.

I asked, "What about the Friends of Al Kufra – Behzad Habibi and the others?" Then I added, "Behzad Habibi – has he talked, Max?"

He said, "Your first question first: when the deal with Teheran's completed, they'll arrange to call off the Friends of Al Kufra. There should be no crossed wires there. That's one view, anyway. There's another. The Friends could be contacted and given a place to make their ambush, the attack on the escort and the freeing of Al Kufra – "

"And all the police forces turning a blind eye? How long before *that* leaks to the press?"

Max drummed his finger-tips on the desk. "Oh, I know, damn it! That's the difficulty, or one of them – "

"Another being the bloodshed. Or is the escort to be instructed similarly? No firing?"

"More or less. Any gunfire to be over their heads. Taken by surprise . . . the bloody man gets away in the confusion."

Obviously, it was to look like a military and police cock-up. They would take the stick afterwards, that being what they were there for. I didn't like any of it; nor, obviously, did Max. It was Spatchcock again, of course. I referred Max back to my second question, Behzad Habibi.

He said, "He's talked a little. Not much. He was brought down from Bradford yesterday. Pentonville. A man from the FO did the questioning, with one of our men present throughout. About all he revealed was what we knew, or believed, already – the IRA involvement. The point was put to him, what use were the Friends of Al Kufra supposed to be to the IRA?"

I asked, "Did he pronounce on that?"

"Yes. Obvious, really. Arms."

"Just that?"

"Yes. Aided by the North Koreans. Aided by Kyoshiro Ka."

"So simple," I said. "Arms, to blow up Stirling Castle. And the Friends have fallen for that, have they?" When Max raised his eyebrows I elaborated. "Aren't the Friends worried that Al Kufra might go up with the castle? Or has the IRA promised to get him out safely – and they've fallen for that too? I don't think they're that dumb, somehow. Do you?"

Max didn't. In fact his advice to Whitehall through Spatchcock had been to go ahead with the shift from Stirling. If that was to be done, then it had to be done fast, before the IRA went into action. The trouble was, Max said, there was procrastination around. No-one seemed willing to commit himself. Al Kufra was too hot a property in the eyes of most of the world. If there was to be a contrived escape, then there must never be any leaks. And because so many people would need to be involved, a leak was inevitable.

Sardonically I made a tongue-in-cheek suggestion. "The best way out would be to concede the Friends' demands. Wouldn't it?"

Max snorted. "Never!" The Prime Minister was adamant on the point. I reflected on hypocrisy. Max's own view was that the best solution would be to allow the IRA to blow up Al Kufra. But that too was out, because of the political set-up, the desire to get on terms with the men in power in Teheran. In any case, no-one wanted anything to happen to Stirling Castle. When I asked about the security there, Max said all that could be done had been or was being done. There was that need for secrecy, so there was no overtly increased police presence, but there was a full alert and the reaction would be fast. Bomb squads and sniffer dogs had been drafted in and there were constant patrols by the normal staff, who were mainly civilians, many of them ex-army or navy. The public had been excluded, the excuse being that reconstruction work was in progress (that was genuine, Max said) and there could be danger from falling masonry. Apart from those of the police and military personnel, virtually the only vehicles allowed entry were tradesmen's vans and builders' lorries.

I asked Max if anything was known as to the current whereabouts of Kyoshiro Ka, the arms dealer. He said nothing was known but he doubted if the man was inside Britain. In any case Max didn't see him as personally important. His arms supply was the important point.

I shrugged and said, "Unfinished business, Max. Operation Tokushima. We never did get Kyoshiro Ka – remember?"

"I remember. But forget it. Concentrate on the present. What do you propose to do now?"

"Shuttle service," I said. "Scene of the action. Back to Glasgow."

"And Stirling Castle?"

"And Stirling Castle," I said.

After a brief word with Felicity I went north again by air, helicopter from the pad on the roof of Focal House to RAF Northolt for a laid-on flight to Glasgow. By arrangement from Focal House an unmarked police car met me and took me straight to Stirling. Coming off the motorway we wound up the steep, cobbled streets towards the castle perched on its commanding rock. I told the driver to go right in. Max had sent word ahead and I was expected. We went over the drawbridge to be stopped at the entry to the courtyard by a civilian custodian in uniform. I produced my 6D2 identity card and said Colonel Anderson was expecting me. I was taken straight to Anderson's office, past the display cabinets bright with the regimental silver, past collections of old Scottish weaponry, broadswords and claymores and highland dirks with silver on their scabbards and cairngorms showing dully at the tops of the small knives and forks thrust into the scabbards for the old-time highland officers to use for eating their meals when in the field. The silver had to be worth a fortune; and it was not silver alone: in the mess as I was taken through I saw, as I'd seen when coming as a guest, the paintings of many distinguished soldiers of the regiment dating back to when, before the Cardwell reforms of 1881, the Argyll and Sutherland Highlanders had been two separate regiments, the 91st and 93rd Regiments of Foot, the 93rd having formed the heroic Thin Red Line at Balaklava in 1854. There was a lot of history around me.

When I was shown into his office, Colonel Anderson got to his feet, apologising for not having met me at the gate. "Thought you wouldn't want that, Commander. The security angle, don't you know."

I agreed: I preferred to be as anonymous as possible. Colonel Anderson took me along to the ante-room, which was otherwise empty, and poured two whiskies. We didn't waste time on too many pleasantries. Anderson asked abruptly if I had any word about the shift to Carlisle and I said I had not. I asked if he thought the castle would prove vulnerable to attack by the IRA.

"Very," he said. "We're doing our best but the place is a rabbit-warren. High explosive could be planted almost anywhere and we'd not know. Unless the dogs sniffed it out . . . and they can be fooled. Obliterative smells, that sort of thing. They're not infallible. I don't like it at all, I can tell you. We look impregnably big and strong but depending on where the explosives are put, and of course the quantity, the damn place could come down like a pack of cards. And what a gloat the IRA would have afterwards – what?"

I agreed. I asked about Al Kufra.

"Little bugger," Anderson said. He was very piqued that his regimental history had been put at risk for a terrorist. "Living off the fat of the land. I understand he's valuable for some reason or other. Had to be kept healthy."

"And comfortable, Colonel?"

Anderson grinned. "No. I wouldn't call it comfortable. Dungeons aren't, especially when ours were built. He's very secure, of course. Armed guards on two-hour changes. Bars and padlocks."

"Exercise?"

"Statutory exercise periods daily, after the construction people have gone."

"A good time for a snatch," I said.

Anderson nodded. "Oh, yes. There was that fellow a few years ago who was snatched from jail by helicopter . . . but our security's good enough, I fancy. When Al Kufra's in the open, we have marksmen stationed on all commanding points around the castle. They have orders to open fire – "

"With helicopters in mind?"

"Yes. But I doubt if these people will try it that way. I'm expecting them to leave it to the IRA."

I said, "That could be fallacious, Colonel. They may be in cahoots up to a point, but the IRA looks after Number One – their own interests." I told him my theories, that the IRA just wanted that supreme prestige target, the castle itself. "We have two enemies to watch for, Colonel, two separate attacks if I'm right – "

"Why don't they make up their minds about Carlisle?" Anderson broke in.

I shrugged. "Same problem. But two castles instead of one. Even if Al Kufra wasn't here, I believe the IRA would still carry on as planned – against Stirling. And the Friends of Al Kufra would see their chance when the convoy was on the road. An ambush."

"Yes, I suppose so." Anderson went off at a tangent then, talking again about the ease with which explosives could be planted. Even outside the walls, he said. If there was enough of it, the walls could be breached near Al Kufra's dungeon and he could be taken out. And a good deal of the castle itself would come down in the process, again if there was enough HE. Thanks to Kyoshiro Ka, although I didn't say this, there certainly would be.

Colonel Anderson asked if I'd like to look at Al Kufra. Did I wish to talk to him? I said I didn't think there would be any point in talking to him but as a matter of curiosity I'd like to see him. Anderson said there was a grille in the door for the use of the guards, who were under orders to look in at frequent but irregular intervals. He took me down to the dungeons, into deep-set gloom and airlessness beneath the massive stone, evil-looking places within the rock itself but vulnerable, Anderson said again, to explosions close against the outer wall. Of course, the perimeter was checked frequently, but, as Anderson said, something could be placed almost at the last minute, and blown quickly either by fuse or remote control.

In a dim light in a passage, I bent and peered through the grille.

I saw Al Kufra sitting on a wooden bench with his head in his hands. After a while he looked up as though he knew he was under scrutiny: it was possible he could see faces behind that grille. The dark face, the glittering eyes – there was an overhead electric light shining down into the dungeon – the swarthiness, the hawk-like features, the face of terrorism, the face of a murderer who killed without compunction, in a detached way, for his fanaticism. It was a commanding face and in its way a handsome one, but it was one without any trace of human feeling in it, a face that would probably show only two emotions, one of scorn, one of anger; plus perhaps one of satisfaction when an act of terrorism had been success-fully completed. Al Kufra was not worth anybody's death in an attempt to preserve him. As we left the dungeon complex Anderson spoke of Al Kufra's record.

"That aircraft business, and so many killings. If he got caught in the cross-fire, as it were, well, it'd be the best thing possible."

I said many people would agree with that but there were considerations that would make his death unacceptable. I didn't elaborate. Colonel Anderson had been a distinguished soldier who in his time had commanded the regiment. He was still in a military environment. He would be disgusted to hear of the Spatchcock plan. I didn't wish to add to his worries and his antipathy for the whole thing. Just before we parted he said, bitterly, that he couldn't see why Al Kufra couldn't be transferred back to a civilian jail, some maximum security prison. I said, non-committally, that there were reasons for

132

not doing that.

"No doubt there are," he said, still bitter. "It's more acceptable to put *us* at risk than other prisoners or prison staff."

I saw his point. But Al Kufra was a fact of life and he was here in Stirling Castle; and here, I reckoned, the authorities would leave him as the thing ran down towards its end. Unless they eventually decided on the idea of an assisted escape from a road convoy. Thinking along those lines an idea came, something to put to the Home Office via Max. But almost at once I rejected it for a very good reason – it had just been an idea that a moment's thought told me had been a bad one. However, to my surprise, when I was back once more in the Glasgow nick I was told that Whitehall had thought of it too and had not rejected it. They were going to act on it; and instructions were on the way to Stirling: Al Kufra was to be left in his dungeon and a decoy road convoy was to leave for Carlisle.

Because the order brooked no argument I made my arrangements but then spoke to Max on the security line. I asked, if an escape was still on the cards à la Spatchcock, why have a decoy which automatically pre-supposed a shoot-out if an ambush came? Why, with the Teheran jiggery-pokery in mind, shoot up the Friends of Al Kufra?

Max was irritable: he hadn't liked any of this from the start. He snapped at me, "The Prime Minister. Don't press me, Shaw. Number Ten's reacted, gone all British. Can't say I cast any blame for that. The new gist of it seems to be bugger Spatchcock. The Friends of Al Kufra have to be flushed out."

"And struck down?"

"That's about it. So – "

I said, "That decoy convoy. I'm going to shadow it. All arrangements made."

"You'll stand out like a bishop entering a brothel!"

"Not so," I said. "An unobtrusive car, call it a fast banger, well maintained. With female passenger embarked. Just for cover – "

"Do you want me to send Miss Mandrake up?" Max cut in with something of a leer in his tone.

"No," I said. "A female CID officer's going to play the part. And look it too." I'd been allocated a young WDC, long blonde hair, well-developed breasts, very casual clothing and all that went with all of that. Max had nothing further to offer; he cut the call. The decoy convoy, I'd been told, was scheduled to leave Stirling Castle that night at eleven p.m. The route would be M80 to the Glasgow ring road, M73 and M74 to A74 for the intersection with the northern end of the M6 where it would turn off onto the A7 for Carlisle. Fast roads all the way, as would be expected if Al Kufra was aboard. I doubted if anything would be tried on the motorway sections; there were better chances along the A74 which wound its way through the remoter areas of Strathclyde and Dumfries and Galloway, across the Southern Uplands and down through Annandale. But I wondered, now, just who it would fool. The Friends of Al Kufra might suspect something like this; but they might still feel it worth the chance of an attack. I didn't imagine it would affect the IRA's plans one way or the other. They would still want Stirling Castle. But one thing was plain: Max had said, bugger Spatchcock. There would be no contrived escape of Al Kufra. Not yet; perhaps that could come, if the proponents of Spatchcockism prevailed on the PM, though I failed to see how an escape could be contrived from the Stirling dungeons. Except, perhaps, by courtesy of the IRA, but that would, of course, be purely fortuitous and scarcely a basis for a plan of campaign.

I had a full session with my allocated WDC. Her name was Jackie; and she was very attractive. Tall and slender and with a smile that lit her face like a beacon, and very direct eyes of blue. I gave her more-or-less the full story, without mentioning the Spatchcock plan and without referring to what was going on in Teheran other than very obliquely. I told her exactly who and what we would be looking out for on the route to Carlisle. I said there might well be shooting. We would both be armed with automatics of heavy calibre and in addition I would have beside me an AK-47 automatic rifle similar to that found in the Glasgow cellars, similar to that used by the IRA. She and I would not join the convoy from the start. An unmarked police car with plain clothes men embarked would follow from the castle to the end of the M80, another would take over until the end of the M74, where it would hand over to us for the run down the lonely stretches of the A74. It should not take us long to pick up any following vehicle. And then we would take it from there, overtaking at times, then falling back.

Jackie asked how word was to be leaked that Al Kufra was on the move. Or said to be.

I said, "They're already expecting a move. No need for a leak. They'll have watchers in Stirling. When the convoy moves out, they'll have their response ready."

"All geared up to go?"

I nodded. The decoy was to be heavily guarded though not overtly so. The term convoy was really a misnomer. There would be no police motor-cycle outriders, no hovering helicopter, no armoured military personnel carriers. Just a police car to lead, and a plain van supposed to contain a manacled Al Kufra. And in fact containing twenty armed police marksmen. Fairly anonymous; but when the vehicles left the castle, there would be something of an act put on. Heavy police presence and the roads in the vicinity coned against parking. That should be enough to alert the Friends of Al Kufra that something important was leaving.

Jackie raised the big query: the one that had made me mentally reject the idea when it had first come to me, the one that I'd asked Max about. She asked, "What, really, is the point, Commander Shaw? I mean . . . you said there was a possibility that there might be a compromise about Al Kufra. So why?"

I said, "Wheels within wheels, Jackie. You're a policewoman. You'll not expect me to . . . shall I say, reveal my sources." I felt pretty mean about that; she was being asked to risk her life without being given all the facts. But that's so often the way of it. Always has been. Pawns have always been expendable, in war and peace. If you could call anything

135

peace when the IRA and the Middle East were involved. It wasn't exactly peaceful in the Province of Ulster. I wondered if the gunmen from the Creggan had yet found the old Irishman's body, whether they knew that I had got away.

13

We picked up the two ex-Stirling vehicles as planned. The timing was to be very exact, and it was. The vehicles came onto the A74 and went past us, and two cars behind them I saw the shadowing car come up. Unobtrusively I took over, dropping into place while the other car went ahead fast and overtook to leave the A74 at the next junction.

There was a fair amount of traffic but I expected it to thin out a lot farther on. The headlights of the cars behind us threw the WDC into relief, making the blonde head shine. That head was down on my left shoulder, Jackie acting the part beautifully. The hair tickled my nose and I sneezed involuntarily.

"Bless you," she said. I apologised. She had a seductive scent and I liked her nearness. But I had above all else to keep alert for trouble. I was watching the traffic behind in my rear-view mirror and I found that Jackie's head was in the way, just a little.

"Slump down a bit," I said, and told her why. She slumped obediently and, dangerously but by way of good cover, I put my arm around her. She seemed to snuggle. I took another look in the mirror: nothing suspicious. I didn't think we had a tail. The ambush, if it was to come, would link in ahead from a side road, any side road, though I'd studied the route in conjunction with Glasgow police and I had a fair idea of where it would be most likely.

We drove on through the darkness, fast, headlights beaming out over open country. There would be hills ahead, and the road would climb, and the van's speed would decrease. It

137

was somewhere in the as yet distant and invisible hills that I expected the trouble to show itself. We had a radio in the car and after a while I switched it on and got an overseas news broadcast from the BBC: I'd often found that the overseas bulletins contained a number of reports that for some reason or other didn't get put on the home news. This time there was a report on Al Kufra. The Prime Minister was determined that the terrorist would not be released or even bargained over and the majority of the cabinet were in agreement. Not all; the Foreign Secretary had demurred – that part was news to me, though hearing it now I could understand. Teheran would not be happy and would react. The BBC put on some sort of expert on Middle Eastern affairs who explained that it was not unlikely that advantage might be gained by the British Government 'reviewing Al Kufra's case' – that was how he put it, as though in quotes. There was no mention of any IRA involvement, no mention of Stirling Castle or of Al Kufra's incarceration there. Of course, the BBC saw a need for care and they were not putting a foot wrong. Fortunately.

Jackie stirred at my side. I said, "Currently there's no-one behind us." I'd checked my rear-view mirror continually throughout. "Sit up if you want to." I added, "You don't have to." But she did so, and gave a low laugh.

She said, "Just to ease the cramp, Commander."

"That all?"

She said a little primly, "We're on duty, sir."

The 'sir' put me in my place. "Sorry," I said, and gave a cough. "It won't occur again." Her response was a giggle. I felt she liked me . . . I switched my thoughts to Felicity Mandrake for a moment. Felicity, safe in Focal House, might well be jealous. I knew she would have been told the score about my shadowing the decoy vehicle and she would be thinking of me, probably, at that moment. Unless she was asleep, of course.

The climb had started; we had reached the hills a while ago and we were now past the turn for Abington. It was a pitch dark night and a drizzle had started. The windscreen was smeared and I gave a touch to the washer. The drizzle increased to a fairly heavy downpour. The wipers swished in front of me. Two cars came up behind and flicked right to pass me on the dual carriageway as I slowed down in time with the decoy van. They went on fast, kicking up a dirty spray. We approached a bend and came round it. Around a hundred yards ahead of the police car and the van a side road joined the A74, coming in left from Crawford. Another car went past, very fast, flinging back more spray.

Jackie said, "There's something in the side road. I think, anyway."

I looked: I got just a glimpse in the headlights – a glimpse of a car in motion. Another car behind it, also moving out. Then as I straightened out of the bend my headlights swung and I lost the cars, but only for a moment or two. When I picked them up again they were emerging from the side road and were coming out to fall in behind the van.

"Suspicious, or not?" Jackie asked.

"I don't know," I answered, "but we'll treat it as such till we find out different. Keep your eyes peeled."

"Will do," she said.

"And your gun handy."

Once again there was nothing behind us. Not until I saw headlights coming up behind, moving very fast, and then a heavy lorry came past us, rushing freight, I supposed, through the night and disregarding speed limits, perhaps for an early London arrival. Keeping in the fast lane it overtook the van. I didn't see whether or not it overtook the police car, but decided it probably wouldn't risk it. It didn't; a moment later I saw it flick left and pull in to come across the decoy van. The van's brake lights glowed, went off again. Then they went on again and through my partly-opened window I heard the scream of the tyres as the brakes went fully on and before I had reacted with some heavy braking of my own I had closed the car next ahead rather faster that I would have liked. Ahead of it I saw in my headlights the lorry pulled half across both lanes.

"This is it," I said as I stopped.

The two cars that had emerged from the side road had now pulled in close to the tailboard of the van. I told Jackie to get out fast and did the same myself. We crouched behind the car and I brought up the AK-47 rifle. Then I saw the tailboard of the van come down with a rush and a rattle and the cargo of police jump down. As they appeared the shooting started from the two cars. I saw four of the police go down, saw the rest scatter. After that I didn't wait; I opened up with the automatic rifle, pouring a long burst towards the cars. Firing came back from them and Jackie gave a cry and went in a sort of stagger towards the roadside. I sent another burst towards the cars and then saw more men coming in from the lorry that had blocked the carriageway. There was more shooting. I slithered across towards where the WDC lay: I found she was dead. She'd taken a bullet through her throat and there had been profuse bleeding. As I straightened and again aimed for the cars and the men from the lorry something happened: there was an explosion and a sheet of flame from the rear of the decoy vehicle. Probably a bullet had entered the petrol tank. The whole scene was lit like day and I saw bodies everywhere, police and the others. And in that blazing light I saw something else, something evil. A very big man, a Japanese built like a wrestler, unmistakably Kyoshiro Ka himself. Just for an instant, then he seemed to vanish. Not for long, however. I had seen no movement; I was concentrating on my other targets. But I felt a presence behind me, felt the muzzle of a gun against my backbone, and heard the voice.

"We meet at last, Commander Shaw."

The rest of it was sheer horror.

They knew they'd been had for suckers when they failed to find Al Kufra and they didn't like it. They had to make a getaway now, and fast. The police car's crew would have radioed in; they were well aware of that. The police car itself was undamaged and one of its crew was still living, though wounded in both hands. So they shot him, in cold blood, a gun held to his head while two other men, dark-skinned men, held his arms. They shot all the other survivors, except me. Then

140

they ran for the lorry and piled aboard, two of them holding me fast. The lorry got on the move, heading south, moving very fast again. It had all been done very quickly, no more than a handful of minutes from start to finish. They'd been lucky; no other traffic, no witnesses. Before long someone would come along and find the wreckage and the carnage. So many bodies, and one of them a young WDC . . .

I felt the lorry turn sharply some way farther along the A74. Presumably the next side road, left. A slip road, probably: soon after, the motion told me we were going round a round-about. We could be crossing over the carriageway to its western side. By this time one of the men had forced my wrists together and applied handcuffs. And I knew there were many guns handy. We drove a long way and there was no pursuit. It was possible, likely in fact, that in the suddenness of the shooting the police car's crew had not been able to pass a full report. The presence of the lorry might not be known.

Out of the lorry, whereabouts I had no idea, I was confronted by Kyoshiro Ka, that man of massive flesh. Thick arms and legs, bloated gut, big heavy face and bald head. The slit eyes stared at me, into me. I was sitting on a hard upright chair, to which I was tied with thin wire that cut into my arms. Around me the room was bare of all furniture except for a clock and the chair. There was a window, heavily curtained. A light hung on a flex, no shade, from a dirty ceiling. The walls were covered with a green wash. The floor was bare wood. Behind me now, the clock ticked, a sound of doom.

Kyoshiro Ka stood in front of me.

"You talk," he said in a voice surprisingly high for so large a man. The sound was like an eunuch.

I said I had nothing to talk about.

He disagreed. "You know everything that is going on."

I laughed. "You flatter me, Kyoshiro Ka. I'm not the Almighty."

"Be serious, please. There is little time. There are things I must know." There was something impressive about the big Japanese, a curious but genuine earnestness that I would not have expected of anyone of his sort. "You do not wish Al Kufra to die."

"Don't I?"

"Your government does not. The death of Al Kufra would be most inconvenient."

"Like the deaths you caused back along the A74," I said. "You've always been a killer, Kyoshiro Ka, whenever you saw the need. All in your own interest, for your rotten arms empire. Am I to take it you're aiming to kill Al Kufra? And if that's the case – why? What's in it for you?"

He looked at me almost sorrowfully, and shook the big bald head from side to side. He said, "You are mistaken, Commander Shaw. I am on your side – "

I laughed at that. "I doubt if you expect me to take that seriously," I said, but he persisted, repeating what he had just come out with. He went on to say, unnecessarily but candidly, that he had no axe to grind for the British government *per se* but there were reasons why he wanted to keep Al Kufra alive. He didn't say why but I could make a fair guess: he himself had a use for the terrorist. Al Kufra could be quite a hostage, the tables turned in a very surprising way. A man like Kyoshiro Ka, with fingers in so many international pies, could bargain in many markets.

He said, "We know that Al Kufra is held in Stirling Castle, Commander Shaw."

"But you were fooled by the decoy."

"Yes. I admit it. In the circumstances, a move seemed so likely. I repeat, we know Al Kufra is in Stirling. That is, he has been. Please tell me if a genuine move to somewhere else is expected to take place."

I said, "I've no idea."

"I think you have. There will be ways of making you talk. You must know that."

"It did occur to me," I said, "but you'll be wasting your time. I genuinely do not know what the Home Office is likely to do next."

He stared at me, broodingly. He had said he was on our side, and he was clearly worried about Al Kufra's safety.

142

There was a strange atmosphere in that bare room, a sort of pregnancy if the word isn't too fanciful, a strong feeling of things about to happen, of events moving to the final throw. I said, "I think you'd better come clean, Kyoshiro Ka. Tell me the whole story. Why not? You seem to be asking my help. Right?"

"Yes, that is right, Commander Shaw."

"Well, then."

So he came out with it, and it wasn't far off what I'd been telling myself. The IRA involvement was turning sour, sour on the man who had been ultimately responsible for the supply of arms and explosives via Libya, notably the Semtex, that very handy plastic agent of destruction. A very large consignment had been delivered and was currently in the hands of the IRA's Belfast Brigade – which was not news to me, of course – and a hit squad was already in Scotland. He knew that because he had many ears in useful places.

I said, "I know all this. The IRA intends to blow Stirling Castle. If they can."

"Yes," he said, "and no."

I was surprised at that. "No? Where does the 'no' come in, then?"

"No, because the Friends of Al Kufra have made known certain things to the IRA, Commander Shaw. If the castle is blown up, it is likely Al Kufra will die – you know this, so do I. So do the Friends of Al Kufra. And so they have told the IRA that if Al Kufra dies, then there will be great enmity from the Middle East, and – "

"And no more arms supplied by – for instance – Libya?"

Kyoshiro Ka nodded. "Or by my organisation."

I laughed. "So the IRA's in a dilemma. Too bloody bad!" I paused. "What have they decided to do about it? Do you know that, Kyoshiro Ka?"

He shook his head. "This I do not know – "

"I'll tell you what I know," I broke in, "and it's this: once Whitehall gets to know of this dilemma business, Al Kufra will stay glued to Stirling Castle for a hell of a long time. And he'll stay alive – which is what you want – isn't it?"

"Yes. And as I have said, it is also what your government wants. But I – " Kyoshiro Ka beat at his massive chest. "I want Al Kufra out!"

"Seems like an impasse," I said.

"Not so. It is on this point that I wish your help. It is not possible for Al Kufra to be snatched from Stirling Castle, this you will agree with, I think. It is a strong place and Al Kufra will be well guarded. Therefore he must be moved – and this time, there will be no subterfuge."

I said he wouldn't have a hope now of extracting Al Kufra by means of a road ambush. "After what happened on the A74 tonight," I said, "any movement would be escorted like gold coming out of Fort Knox."

Kyoshiro Ka smiled, a smile of confidence. "Not, perhaps. If your government understands where its best interests lie, not. I think you understand me, Commander Shaw?"

I believed I did. The Japanese was suggesting something along the lines proposed by Spatchcock and now apparently rejected by the Prime Minister. An assisted escape . . . there might be attractions yet in that, and never mind the Prime Minister, whom I now knew to have been opposed by the Foreign Secretary. But if that were to be done, the Spatchcock plan re-activated, there were other dangers. Once Al Kufra was away, then Stirling Castle would be at risk from the IRA. But of course the castle itself was of no concern to Kyoshiro Ka. The deaths caused to civil and military personnel wouldn't register with him. A very big cleft stick loomed for Whitehall once all this became known. I asked Kyoshiro Ka what he expected me to do about it. He then went into a longish spiel. He knew, of course, all about Focal House; his organisation had fought us in the work-out of Operation Tokushima. He knew our power and influence and the way we worked outside government but with its full co-operation; he knew we were a much trusted outfit throughout the non-communist world. He knew just what Max could do and get away with. He knew we often turned a blind eye to the law, and that the law turned a blind eye to us just as often.

"Verbiage," I said. "What about the nub of all that, something concrete?"

"Yes," he said, and the hard core emerged. Put bluntly, it was perfectly simple. I was to speak to Max personally; Kyoshiro Ka had some sophisticated radio equipment that could tap into the Focal House frequencies, the supposedly secure frequencies that would not, or should not, be tappable by anyone. And I was to advise Max that Al Kufra should be moved – where, didn't matter, just so long as Max came back to me with the route to be taken and details of the escort. I was also to suggest that Al Kufra should be allowed that assisted escape. Very easy: in fact all I had to do was say to Max that I advised the Spatchcock plan. That was all. And, of course, I was not to say anything else at all. No mention, for instance, of the IRA and Stirling Castle. But that part of it was known to Whitehall already, so the situation in that respect was unchanged. If things went Kyoshiro Ka's way, Stirling – not just the castle probably, but the surrounding area, well populated, as well – would be shattered. I recalled what Colonel Anderson had said: that the planting of explosives would be easy, with all the construction work going on.

"You will be most cautious in what you say to Max," Kyoshiro Ka said, quiet but ominous. "You will be convincing in your advice – "

I said, "There's just one thing. I don't propose to do it, Kyoshiro Ka. I'm not going to foul up – whatever it may be that Whitehall's considering."

The eyes glittered. "That is final?"

"It's final."

"I think it is not," he said softly. I awaited whatever method he used to make men talk, comply with his wishes. But there was no rough stuff. Nothing physical. Still speaking softly he said, "Late last night there was a telephone call to Focal House. The call was from the Metropolitan Police. Miss Mandrake's flat had been ransacked. The police wished her to attend because there was evidence that the ransacking had been done by the Friends of Al Kufra. Focal House checked the call back and found that it was genuine. It was also genuine that the Friends of Al Kufra acting on my instructions

145

had indeed been the ransackers. Miss Mandrake was taken to her flat under escort from Focal House. When Miss Mandrake got out of the car she was seized and her escort and driver were shot. This happened a little after midnight, Commander Shaw."

My mind was in a turmoil now. At that time I'd been on the road with the WDC, behind the decoy vehicle. I asked through dry lips, "Where is she now?"

"For the present, in safety. And unharmed. Such may not last. Now I think you will call Max."

14

I called Max on Kyoshiro Ka's equipment, to which, still
wired to the chair, I was carried – it was set up in an adjoining
room. Max and Whitehall didn't have to take my advice after
all, though I reckoned Max probably would. But it wouldn't
really be my decision – so I told myself in order to ease my
conscience. In effect, I would be doing no more than giving
him the truth of the current situation and both he and
Whitehall – and Spatchcock – could take it from there. I
didn't feel all that bad about it as I heard his voice coming
through in response to my call. And his first words confirmed
what Kyoshiro Ka had said: Felicity had been taken.

As ordered by Kyoshiro Ka, I feigned startled surprise. I
didn't need to fake the anxiety. Max told me not to worry; she
would be got back, which I didn't believe. Then, dismissing
Felicity, he asked what I had to report.

"I'm not in a position to say much," I said as Kyoshiro Ka
prodded at me warningly with a small automatic. "Just this: I
have good reason to offer certain advice. An assisted escape."
On reflection I had decided not to mention Spatchcock in
Kyoshiro Ka's hearing; to him, Spatchcock could be some sort
of code word and he might react dangerously. I carried on
with what I had to say to Max, which was that for his own
safety Al Kufra should be on the move soonest possible. I
made it sound very urgent.

It was Max who came out with it: he said, "The Spatchcock
plan – is that it?" and I said yes, it was. Then Max went on to
tell me something interesting and very relevant: the Foreign
Secretary had gained cabinet support and the Prime Minister

was becoming subject to a possible change of mind. Teheran was more important after all. Thus the ground work for an escape had been started already. It had already been decided in fact to shift Al Kufra again, this time for real. He would leave Stirling for Perth jail at midnight that night under a strong escort. At the same time there would be another decoy, equally strongly guarded, leaving Stirling Castle for Barlinnie in Glasgow.

I asked what the route to Perth would be. Max said, "M9 to Dunblane, A9 past Greenloaming and Blackford and into Auchterarder where the convoy will turn off onto the B8062 for Dunning, Forteviot and Bridge of Earn for Perth, which avoids going through the city centre – the A9 comes in at the other end of Perth from the jail." He paused. "For Spatchcock purposes it's a good route – plenty of twists and turns. Fair for ambush."

When Max asked for full details of the A74 slaughter, Kyoshiro Ka did something to the transceiver and there was a lot of atmospheric interference and we went off the air. To Max, it would have sounded just like a bum connection.

Kyoshiro Ka asked, "What is this Spatchcock?"

I said, "Oh, just – Spatchcock. Man from Whitehall, who's given certain advice in the past."

Kyoshiro Ka wasn't slow in the uptake. "To allow the escape, to save face?"

He knew; I said that was correct. That pleased him a lot. He said that in that case the matter should now move smoothly ahead. Also, he said, he knew the B8062. There couldn't be a better road for his purpose. I found it a weird situation: Whitehall and Kyoshiro Ka were seeing things from a shared viewpoint. But I wondered how the Friends of Al Kufra were going to react to Kyoshiro Ka's self-interested treachery.

Rather badly, I imagined. Which was an interesting thought.

The time was 0900 hours: Max would have remained over-night in his penthouse suite after being given news of the shoot-out on the A74. Kyoshiro Ka put on the BBC News and I heard the report. It was fairly brief, just the bare facts, the many bodies, the burned-out van. There was no mention of Al Kufra or of the purpose of the police-filled vehicle that had been ambushed. There was a blackout on all reference to Al Kufra, had been for a while now. Likewise, there was no mention of Stirling Castle or the IRA.

Kyoshiro Ka switched the radio off. I asked again about Miss Mandrake.

"Be patient," was the answer. Soon after this Kyoshiro Ka left the premises. Two men, North Koreans, were left on guard and I remained wired up on that hard chair. Food and water were brought and I was allowed a visit to the lavatory after drinking the water, the wire remaining on my body but unsecured from the chair. The rest of the time they sat watching me, each with an automatic ready. They didn't speak and I didn't waste breath on questions that I knew wouldn't be answered. I was very conscious of the ticking of the clock on the wall.

I did a lot of thinking, trying to assess the future. In the circumstances of the IRA's sudden and enforced concern for Al Kufra's life, it was obvious that their attack on Stirling wouldn't manifest at least until after midnight, but that didn't give anybody a lot of scope. I reasoned that the blow-up would come by remote control, somewhere in the town below the castle. The charges would already be set. There would have been thorough body searches of all personnel entering, the construction workers included, but the Semtex could have been brought in much earlier, by members of the public, sightseers at that time unsuspected – American tourists even, supporters of NORAID before the clamp-down and the searches. They could have been cleverly concealed for days past, and then planted in the vital spots by the construction workers whose ranks could have been easily enough infiltrated by the IRA. It seemed to me that Stirling Castle had had it once Al Kufra was out.

The room I was in remained curtained and I couldn't see the clock so I didn't know what time it was when Kyoshiro Ka returned from whatever he'd been doing, which was, he said, making his arrangements for the forthcoming ambush. He was full of confidence, not unreasonably after the success of the night before. He had no fear of the British police.

I asked again, "Where's Miss Mandrake?"

The answer was the same: "Be patient, Commander Shaw."

I was rattled; had been, all day. I said, "I want to know what you're doing with her. I want to know if she's safe."

"She is safe, yes. So long as you continue to do your part for us, she will remain safe."

I asked what else was wanted of me. I was told that I was to accompany the ambush, the highway snatch of Al Kufra. When I asked why, Kyoshiro Ka didn't answer. Maybe he just wanted me to be gunned down – he wouldn't have forgiven me for the Tokushima business, and however 'assisted' the escape might be there would inevitably be casualties. A neat revenge; gunned down by my own side.

I believe we could not have been far from Stirling. It was 2200 hours before things started moving. I heard the sound of vehicles beyond that curtained window. Kyoshiro Ka went outside and came back within a couple of minutes.

"All is ready," he said. He was very confident but there was an edge of nervous tension as the climax of all his efforts began its approach. He gave an order to the guarding gunmen and I was unwired from the chair and my arms were at last free. The relief was enormous but the first movements were painful; it took quite a while for the circulation to return fully. Kyoshiro Ka waited impatiently. At his order one of the guards massaged my arms and that helped. When I was ready I was taken from the room. It was pitch dark outside, no lights at all from the house or from the vehicles, which I could see only dimly. There were two of them, and I made them out as my eyes grew night-accustomed: a big car, a Citroën, and, inevitably, a van. The back of the van was open and inside I made out a number of legs, men seated on benches fore and aft. Behind my back Kyoshiro Ka flicked on a torch, briefly, and I saw the dull gleam of weapons, more of the AK-47 assault rifles, the quickfirers. Just a glimpse, then I was pushed towards the Citroën and told to get in the back.

There were two other persons in the back. One was an armed North Korean. The other was Felicity. I spoke to her.

"No talking," the armed man said. Another man got in with us; four in the back could have been a squeeze, but the North Koreans were small and Felicity was slender. Kyoshiro Ka got in the front passenger seat. He exuded confidence still. What neither he nor I knew at that stage was that Max had smelled a very big rat as a result of my call to him on Kyoshiro Ka's radio equipment.

Kyoshiro Ka gave the word and we started off, pulling out from a concreted drive-in that ran round in the rear of what I saw in the headlights was a big square stone-built house, very run-down and with broken windows. The concrete was cracked in places and weeds grew in the cracks. From the drive we turned to the left, and went ahead at a moderate speed with around a hundred yards between the vehicles.

After a while Kyoshiro Ka turned round and issued orders. The ambush would take place just around a sharp corner on the last stretch of the convoy's route from Stirling, on the B8062. The two vehicles would be concealed in a lay-by, a sector of disused roadway cutting off another sharp bend. There was good tree cover between the lay-by itself and the new bit of road.

But the attack would not come immediately and might not come at all. That was to depend upon me.

The Citroën and then the van slowed and turned off into the yard of what looked and smelled like a byre, an apparently disused one.

I was told to get out. My personal gunman came close behind me and another emerged from the byre itself. He, too, was a Korean. I was led into the byre, which a moment later was lit by Kyoshiro Ka's torch. The ground was filthy, ankle deep in straw and manure, and there was a sort of manger standing empty. I didn't think the previous occupant had been long gone; anyway, the cow smell lingered. I was told to take off my outer clothing. Other clothing including wellies was produced from a cardboard box and a canvas bag. I was given this clothing and told to dress. I emerged in the guise of a chief superintendent of police, silver-edged cap and all, and thus clad was ordered back into the car with Felicity, to whom I had still not been allowed to speak, and we got on the road again. The police uniform fitted where it touched but would probably pass muster on a dark road on a dark night; the too-short trousers tucked neatly into the wellingtons.

I was given my orders by Kyoshiro Ka.

"The convoy with Al Kufra will slow considerably on the approach to the bend," he said. "You will show yourself as the leading vehicle slows down. You will bring the convoy to a halt . . . and you will remember that all the rest of us will be in the lay-by. With Miss Mandrake. You understand?"

I understood very well about Felicity and what might happen to her. But I didn't yet see in detail the part I was to play. I said so.

When Kyoshiro Ka gave me the answer it sounded simple enough. I was to say that orders had been received by Perth police, in whose patch the convoy would by then be, that I was to take over Al Kufra. Once Max had acted on my call to him the officer in charge of the escort would have had his own orders as to a contrived escape and would understand.

"There should be no difficulty," Kyoshiro Ka said. "Unless it is made by yourself, Commander Shaw." His next words were ominous but not unexpected. "I shall be close and listening. If you say anything at all that you should not – you understand me, I think – then Miss Mandrake dies. And the convoy is attacked. So many unnecessary deaths . . . if either you, or Focal House, or your government, reneges on the arrangements made."

"You cover everything, don't you," I said in a flat tone, sick now with worry.

He laughed. "It is to that that I attribute my success in life," he said.

We moved on, coming through a small town and then again

152

out into open country. In the headlights' beam I looked out on trees and isolated buildings like barns, and the occasional farm, and hills. A very peaceful scene. There was scarcely any traffic. Another small town, and a number of drunks leaving a pub in the main street. They were singing loudly and in maudlin fashion, and I identified 'Loch Lomond'. They took not the slightest notice of the vehicles. But the words of the song took on a nightmare quality for me. *But me and my true love will never meet again . . .*

Was Felicity my true love? I didn't really know; I'd not led the sort of life where one settles down with a true love. Together we'd been through so many dangers for 6D2, dangers similar to this one, but this time Kyoshiro Ka had it all sewn up so far as I could see. Once he'd got his hands on Al Kufra he *might* let Felicity go free. Me too. But I doubted it. There was that personal angle, the revenge that lay in him for Tokushima. He would never pass up the chance.

Some way along the B road after passing through Forteviot we slowed, as would the convoy in due course, for that bend. It was very sharp, due any time, probably, for straightening.

We rounded it and there was the lay-by with its concealing trees. As might have been expected perhaps there was already a car in it as the Citroën pulled off the road. The headlights slammed into it with full brilliance and I caught a glimpse of two startled heads looking round through the rear screen. Someone was having it away and they didn't like the intrusion.

Kyoshiro Ka was not at all worried. "Keep on the headlights," he said to the driver, "and they will go quickly."

They did. They went with a speed that showed their anger, stones and grit flying back from the tyres. Then we waited, and Kyoshiro Ka began whistling through his teeth. He sounded happy. He kept a sharp eye on the clock in the Citroën's console.

15

As the estimated time of arrival of the road convoy drew near, Kyoshiro Ka went with me to stand in the cover of the trees, close to the main road. My throat felt dry, thinking of Felicity still in the car with the armed men. Kyoshiro Ka was armed with an automatic and there was another man behind me, also ready with a gun, inevitably an AK-47.

Time passed; Kyoshiro Ka kept on looking at the luminous dial of his wrist-watch. The convoy was later than he had expected. Twice vehicles passed by us, but they were nothing to do with Al Kufra.

Kyoshiro Ka became restive.

"If there is lying from Focal House . . ." He didn't finish the sentence; but he didn't need to.

I asked, "What if the convoy doesn't come? What do you do then?"

He said, "I wait for the IRA to blow up the castle."

"And lose Al Kufra."

He shrugged at that. He gave no answer. Perhaps it was the case that if he couldn't have Al Kufra himself, then the terrorist would be better dead where no-one could have him – I just didn't know what was going on in Kyoshiro Ka's mind. I wondered, as we waited in that thick darkness with a few moments later a cold wind getting up, just how much Max knew that he hadn't told me when I'd made that call to Focal House from Kyoshiro Ka's radio set-up, just what Max might be contriving even now. I shivered in the cold wind, which was increasing. From somewhere close at hand an owl hooted, three times. The first hoot had made me jump: my nerves

154

were at full stretch. Under my breath I cursed all owls. There was a feeling of Macbeth in the air, a feeling that the trees might move towards Dunsinane and three witches make a sudden appearance with a smoking cauldron, that the lay-by would turn into a blasted heath.

It was another ten minutes by Kyoshiro Ka's watch before we heard the convoy's approach, or what we both took to be the convoy. A heavy sound, and a number of headlights beaming into the bend and off the trees, obviously not just one single vehicle such as had passed us earlier on those two occasions. We had a good view of the bend as the approaching vehicles came round slow, in low gear.

There was a police car in the lead.

"Now," Kyoshiro Ka said in my ear.

I stepped out into the road, clearly visible in the headlights, and waved the police car down.

It stopped, and a sergeant got out.

"What's going on, sir?" he called.

"Perth police," I said.

"Aye, sir. Is there something up?"

"I have orders to take over the prisoner."

He said, "Oh-ah," and seemed uncertain, naturally so. His personal anxiety was relieved when someone got down from the vehicle next in rear and came towards us. I saw the uniform of a prison officer and behind it again an army uniform also approaching. I saw the crowns of a major. It was the major who did the talking.

"What's all this?"

I said my piece again as the major came up. He said, "We've had certain orders. No doubt you understand."

"I do," I said.

"I suppose this is some sort of cock-up," the major said. I didn't follow; but I felt the watchful presence of Kyoshiro Ka behind the trees, and the van full of armed men, and Felicity in the car. Cock-ups didn't help my particular situation. I asked, "Why a cock-up?"

The major gave a short laugh like a sudden bark. He said, "It happens in the armed forces. Did you ever hear the story of

155

the naval officer who lived in Portsmouth and received orders to proceed to Colombo to join HMS *Southampton*, and – "

"I've heard it," I said, arriving at the facts. "I've had . . . naval connections myself. When the officer got to Colombo, he found he should have reported down the line to Southampton to join HMS *Colombo*."

"Got it in one," the major said. "I suppose you weren't kept fully genned up, Chief Superintendent. Awfully sorry and all that. The person concerned has gone to Barlinnie. Should be there by now. I'm afraid you've had a trip for nothing." He gave me a wave and went back with the prison officer towards his vehicle. The police sergeant got back into his car. I stood there like a dummy for a few moments. It wasn't until later that I learned that this was the result of Max having smelled that rat after my radio telephone call. For the present there were other things to worry about, much closer things.

Either Kyoshiro Ka hadn't heard the verbal exchanges or if he had he hadn't believed the major, putting his words down to chicanery on the part of the British authorities. Whatever it was, he went into his attack as initially planned. It was done with ferocious suddenness, the occupants of the van coming out fast from the lay-by and spreading right across the roadway and down the flanks. A murderous fire was opened in an instant. The major and the prison officer went down in pools of blood before the convoy drivers reacted and doused their headlights. A swathe of fire from the AK-47 took the police car and colandered it, and it went up in a sheet of flame, cremating the sergeant and his driver. Troops and police jumped down from an armoured personnel carrier and began returning the fire. This being not the real convoy, they were not there in strength. They were there simply to put on a convincing show, presumably, when the fake convoy had left Stirling. They were outnumbered by the men from Kyoshiro Ka's van; it looked like being a massacre on a similar scale to that on the A74. Or almost: the survivors scrambled back into the personnel carrrier and a moment later I heard the chatter of a machine gun and bullets zipped past me. Kyoshiro Ka was still behind me with his gun in my back; he caught a bullet and spun round with a howl of pain. He dropped the gun; I picked it up and slammed the barrel down hard on his forehead and he staggered and fell. With all the men from the van engaged in the shoot-out, I ran back fast into the lay-by and made for the Citroën. I saw Felicity in the back. With her now was one of the North Koreans. I saw he had a gun. He fired through the rear screen, which shattered. His aim was poor. Mine was better: I got his gun hand and heard his howl of pain like Kyoshiro Ka's earlier. As I came right up to the Citroën I saw Felicity's head duck down: she was going for the gun.

I flung myself into the driving seat and got moving, exiting from the other end of the lay-by, out onto the road for Perth. I asked Felicity if she was all right and she said, breathlessly, that she was.

"And our friend?"

"Quiescent," she said. "Where are you heading?"

"Perth," I said. "Police. Then a call to Stirling Castle. There'll be a lot of people at risk there from now on." I didn't say any more; I concentrated on my driving. There would probably be a pursuit. It could be police and military or it could be the remnants of Kyoshiro Ka's force in the van. That depended on who won out behind, and I fancied it was going to be Kyoshiro Ka. However, the van wouldn't have the speed of the Citroën and I should be able to make Perth in time.

Should.

But it didn't work out that way.

I heard Felicity's sudden cry from the back and then I felt the Korean's gun-muzzle pressing into the bone behind my left ear.

I had been ordered to turn and go back the way we had come. The gun had been removed from my neck and I knew Felicity was once again at first risk. So I made a three-point turn. I drove back towards the lay-by and what would be left of the convoy. I thought again about Stirling Castle and its environs. I reckoned there was time in hand yet, if any use could now be made of it. I didn't expect the IRA to go into their explosive action until after daylight, probably in, say, mid-morning when there would be more people around to be killed. I was no longer bothered about Al Kufra; it could be presumed he was safe in Barlinnie jail in Glasgow. But it did seem as though the Spatchcock plan had died the death this time.

Meanwhile there was the danger ahead. At any moment I expected to see the van coming down on us. The next time we met up with Kyoshiro Ka would be the end, presumably; he was going to be very vindictive now. I watched the road – no sign yet of the opposition, no headlights to slice the darkness of a dirty night – it was raining now, and the wipers were going.

I heard Felicity's rapid breathing. She'd been through too much recently and now there was nothing I could do to help. But I knew I had to act fast and take a big chance. A chance on her life as well as mine. I had that certainty another encounter that night with Kyoshiro Ka's outfit would be very final and I decided, almost in cold blood, to take that chance, that last chance as I saw it, the chance that could go either way. Not surprisingly in the circumstances, the others had not bothered with seat belts and when, with a clear stretch of road ahead of me, I virtually stood on the brakes, both Felicity and the Korean were taken off guard.

I felt the impact of Felicity's body against the back of my seat and then the gunman's head came through the gap between the front seats. As I tried to control the skid I'd gone into on the greasy wet road, I got an arm around the man's neck and held him fast. The Citroën shot across the road and into some trees. There was snapping and crackling all around us and then the car tilted sharply and began a very nasty sideways slither. We'd gone over a slope behind the trees.

We landed upside down, with my arm still around the Korean. I thought at first that I'd broken his neck, but then I felt him struggle.

We were all alive, and the chance had paid off. So far. I scrambled clear; the results of the skid had bashed in the doors on the offside and then torn them off their hinges. I pulled Felicity clear. She was very badly shaken up and had a number of cuts and bruises but otherwise she was intact. As for me, I'd been saved by my seat belt. The gunman was in poor shape: both arms were broken and he was beginning to moan. I pulled him out from the wreckage unceremoniously and dumped him on the leaves and earth and stones. His face was covered with blood, and more blood dripped from the hand I'd shot. There was no fight left in him. I got down and foraged about in the car's interior until I had found the gun, a heavy calibre revolver.

Felicity asked what we did next. Her voice was very shaky.

I said, "Frankly, I don't know yet."

"Contact the police . . ."

"Yes," I looked around: how to contact the police was a good question . . . I gave myself a mental shake: of course, they'd be along soon. That murderous shoot-up was not going to go unnoticed. It was possible the armoured personnel carrier had had radio contact with Stirling. On the other hand, there had certainly been nothing coming along the road.

I said, "We reconnoitre for a start. See if Kyoshiro Ka's on his way." It was then that I heard a vehicle moving along the road above and beyond the slope. I heard it stop. There would be plenty of evidence of something having crashed into and through the trees, and there would be the skid marks and the marks of very heavy braking.

"Could be police," I said. "It could also be someone else. Until we're sure, keep as quiet as you can."

I took her hand in mine, then put an arm around her. She was shivering as though she would never stop. I held her tight. We waited for whatever was going to happen. The Korean had stopped moaning. I released Felicity and bent down to him. He had passed out; there was probably damage to his head, a nasty blow or some such. I felt for his heart; he was alive if only just.

Now there were sounds of movement from above, a pushing through broken branches and undergrowth. Next I saw the beam of a torch, silvering the trees. I fancied there were several persons up there and they were coming in a wide spread. More minutes passed; we kept very quiet but I knew,

159

now, that they couldn't miss us. Whoever 'they' were.

The sounds, the crunching, came closer. So did the torch –
more than one torch. As the beam of one of the torches cut
across through the trees it lit on a man. Two men. Not police,
not any of Kyoshiro Ka's bunch, no dark or yellow skins
though I could have been mistaken about that. But I wasn't.

The torch lit on us. We would have been very clearly seen. I
heard a voice. "Police." They'd seen the chief superintendent's uniform. More torches. Then another voice from behind the beams. "It's them, be Jesus! Him, anyway. The
bloody Brit."

They came closer from all sides, moving in. One of them
began whistling. The tune was 'The Belfast Brigade'.

16

There were six of them. One of them asked about the police get-up: I said he'd better ask Kyoshiro Ka. I recognised the men from the Creggan in Londonderry. I recognised the young man, Seamus. One of them said, "So you got away. From the old man."

"Have you just realised that?" I asked sarcastically.

"No. Oh, no. We'd have dealt with the old man, had he not blown his face off for himself. He knew what'd be coming to him, all right."

We were surrounded by the guns. One of the men looked down at the Korean. "Who's this?"

Another man enlightened him. "One of the Jap's bunch." The speaker aimed a vicious kick at the still unconscious man, who started moaning again and stirred a little. "The bastards think only of themselves after all," the man said.

"And we have to think of the arms, Kevin. The supply."

"Ach, I know that." The man addressed as Kevin turned his attention to me. He jerked his gun towards Felicity. "Who's this, then?" he asked. "The lady friend, is it?"

I said, "Yes." If he didn't know Felicity's role in life, I wasn't going to tell him. "She got involved."

"Oh, yes?" There was a laugh. "You're a fine man, then, to involve the girl friend. If that's all she is, which I somehow find myself doubting. What are you doing here, the two of you, with the Jap's sidekick? Will you tell me that, you bloody Brit?"

I shrugged. "Why not? If you've come from the Stirling direction, you'll have seen what happened back along the road."

"We have, yes. So where's Al Kufra now?"

I didn't answer directly. I took a chance on the man's apparent ignorance of the facts and said, "Kyoshiro Ka – you know of him?"

"Yes, we do. So?"

I settled for the truth. For all I knew, these men could have had words with Kyoshiro Ka already. "Kyoshiro Ka ambushed the convoy. But there was no Al Kufra."

"I asked, where is he now?"

"In Stirling Castle," I said, leaving the truth behind now. It was about the only way of delaying what was going to happen.

"How do you know this?"

"I spoke to the officer in charge of the convoy, which was a decoy."

The men went into a huddle of whispered conversation. Rain dripped from the surrounding trees and the wind blew cold, rustling the leaves. Felicity was shivering more than ever. There was quandary in the air, in the minds of the gunmen from Ulster. Then they came out of their huddle and I was addressed again by Kevin. "You'll come with us. I warn you, don't give any trouble. And keep your mouths shut."

The guns closed in, two to me, two to Felicity. The other two picked the Korean up and carried him between them. We were pushed ahead of the guns through the trees, up the slope and back to the roadway. There was a minibus drawn into the cover of the trees, well hidden from the road, and behind the wheel was the girl, Deidre. I saw in the torchlight, briefly before the torch was doused as we came clear of the trees, that the minibus had the name of an oil company painted along its side, an American company with an Aberdeen address. We all piled in through the rear doors and then Kevin gave the word to go. Deidre started off, back along the road towards Auchterarder and Stirling. We came past the scene of the ambush. Before we reached it, I had seen the lights and the cones ahead. The police were there now. They gave us only a cursory glance and we were waved on past. Some of the carnage had been cleared up but the road looked slippery with

162

blood. Bodies were laid out in a neat row by the side of the road, not yet covered. Among them I saw the huge, bloated form of Kyoshiro Ka. He wouldn't be causing any more trouble; that, I thought, spelled the end at long last of Operation Tokushima, but currently that didn't seem very important.

A little before Forteviot I saw headlights and then a series of blue flashes. Three ambulances went past us at speed. A little late.

On the A9 dual carriageway the minibus took the Auchterarder bypass. We passed the turn for Blackford in the Braes of Ogilvie and after passing Greenloaning we entered Dunblane. The man Kevin began singing in a low voice. The one about the girl and the wicked, carnal priest who 'into bed laid her, and now yon wee lassie's the whore o' Dunblane . . .'

Leaving the M9 after the A9 we pulled into Stirling along a road of down-market shops. The Scottish weather had now changed again and there was a moon appearing now and again through the cloud cover. That moon lit on the high walls and pinnacles of the castle, darkly gaunt in the night. The town lay sleeping beneath its once protective presence. It would be a shattering business in more ways than the one when the IRA went into the final act. A thousand years of Scottish history would be gone; something impregnable to Scottish hearts would die forever. If the IRA could hit at Stirling Castle they could hit anything at will, and what would be the next target? No-one in Stirling, no-one in all Scotland other than those charged with his safety, would be concerned about Al Kufra who wasn't even there. But Whitehall was going to get plenty of stick for not preserving the great castle. Again I thought about the people who would be at work there after daylight had come, the guides and wardens, the staff of the regimental headquarters and the museum; and of those irreplaceable treasures of the Argylls. There was a lot of affection for the regiment in Scotland.

The one thin thread of hope lay in Kevin and his gunmen believing that Al Kufra was still inside. They wouldn't be

163

taking any chances. The orders from Sinn Fein, the political masters of the IRA, would have been precise: the continuing arms supply was the most important issue.

The minibus climbed towards the castle. Just a little way. It stopped on the slope and Deidre left it in gear and pulled the handbrake hard on. Right alongside us was the entry to a dark, narrow alley; and the minibus had been stopped close to it, the wheels on the pavement. We were ordered out through the side door and straight into the alley. When the Korean gunman had been carried out, a man emerged from a doorway giving onto the alley and got into the vehicle. Deidre handed over to him and joined the rest of us. The minibus was driven away, up towards the castle but before I was pushed through the doorway I saw it coming back down the hill again after turning higher up.

I went into an unlit passage, feeling my way along the walls. When the outer door was shut a light came on overhead. I saw stairs at the end of the passage. Felicity and I were told to go on up. Off the first landing four doors opened. We were hustled through one of them. There was a plain wooden table and a number of chairs. There was a central light, unshaded, hanging from the ceiling. The window was curtained.

We were told to sit. The Korean had not been brought up.

The gunmen sat also. Kevin said, "We wait for Riley. Riley, the man of truth. The man of destiny."

After that there was no more talk. The gunmen just sat there looking expressionless, as did Deidre. Kevin pulled a packet of cigarettes from a pocket. He lit up without offering the packet round. We waited for Riley, man of truth and destiny. We waited a long while. Eventually I saw the curtains lighten with the dawn. A while longer and then Kevin got up and drew the curtains aside after switching off the light. I saw that the window was heavily barred outside.

Then there was a ring of a bell from down below and Kevin said, "Ah now, that'll be Riley. Go down and let him in, Deidre."

The girl left the room. She came back with a stunted figure wearing a black patch over one eye. I wondered in which of

164

many gun battles Riley had lost that eye, how many British soldiers and members of the RUC had died by his hand. Riley had a dangerous face, the look of a killer and a fanatic, a slit for a mouth and a nasty, smouldering look in the one eye.

Kevin said, "Well now, Riley."

"Al Kufra's out. He's in Barlinnie jail."

"You're sure, Riley?" There was excitement in the tone.

"I am certain sure," the man of truth said firmly.

The look on Kevin's face said clearly that it was now all systems go. It said also that he didn't like the fact I'd misinformed him about Al Kufra. He said I was going to suffer for that.

Kevin left the room with Riley and four of the others. Deidre was left behind with us. So was Seamus. They both had guns, of course. I didn't doubt that they would use them; the revolvers carried silencers and a few phuts wouldn't penetrate next door. Just to assure us on the point of no-one hearing, Deidre remarked that the adjoining properties were empty and had been for some while.

"Which is why we chose this place," she said. She stared at Felicity; had been staring at her, in fact, on and off ever since we'd been brought to the room. "You've good taste in women, Commander Shaw."

"Thank you," I said.

"Better she stays looking like she does," Deidre said.

I got the underlying threat. Good looks could vanish fast in the hands of those inclined to spoil them. I said, "She needs a doctor. You can see that for yourself, can't you?"

"There'll be no doctors coming here," Deidre said with flat finality. She gave her hair a toss. "It's too late anyway."

"Too late?"

"That's what I said."

I asked, "When's zero hour?"

"For the castle?" Deidre looked at Seamus as if for guidance.

Seamus said carefully, "It doesn't matter now. As you said, it's too late." He spoke to me. "The explosives will be

165

detonated at 1130 hours this morning."

It was now a little after eight. "No warning?" I asked.

"No warning, no. Why should there be?"

I shrugged. "You do, sometimes. A matter of humanity."

Seamus laughed, so did Deidre. Seamus said, "Humanity be buggered. They're all Brits in there."

Obviously.

I said, "We all speak the same language."

"Only because you Brits imposed it on us."

"And we have the same traditions. Broadly."

"Balls," Seamus said.

A philosophical discussion was evidently not a strong urge with Seamus. It wasn't with me either. I just wished the whole lot would fry in hell. They probably would, one day. They didn't represent Ireland, as the old man in Portsalon had said. God, I reckoned, would sort them out from the true patriots of what they didn't like being called John Bull's Other Island. I tried one more question, since Seamus didn't seem to mind.

I asked, "Where's the detonation to be activated from?"

"Not from here," he said. He said that with a scowl on his face, and after a slight hesitation. Did I, I wondered, detect a touch of unease . . . maybe of something having gone a little wrong? It was a tempting thought but really it was no more than that.

I said brightly, "Let's talk about the weather, shall we?"

"Bugger the weather," Seamus answered. He clammed up after that and we sat in silence. Perhaps we were once again waiting for Riley.

They came for us around two hours later, after a visit apiece, under guard, to a bathroom on the same landing as the prison room. I was tempted on that visit to pull the bathroom trick again, as I had done in the subterranean regions of the Glasgow warehouse; but the circumstances were different and Kevin and his gunmen, plus Riley, were handy for retaliation and we wouldn't have a hope. I had to wait for a better moment. The thing was far from over yet, though the time was running down fast. There might come a way but if there was

166

one lurking in the wings I certainly couldn't see it. In the meantime I was very worried about Felicity; she'd hit her head during that skid down the slope and she was very pale. The gashes and bruises were puffed as if with poisoning from the earth that had got into them. She was still shivering.

Too late to worry, Seamus had said. I supposed it was. It was clear enough that we would both be disposable after the blow-up and disposed of we would be. It was a time for prayer rather than anything else. Under pressure of events, I did my best. I wondered, after prayer, what Max would be doing after hearing of the second ambush and me not contacting since. There wouldn't be much he could do about us, of course . . .

It was Riley who came for us. Riley, looking more murderous than before and with news to impart. The go was now, he said. And there had been a shift of plan, a last minute thing. Something had leaked; or if it hadn't, then the Brits were playing safe. Stirling Castle was being evacuated. "They'll not get them all away," he said, "but we're advancing the time nevertheless. Downstairs, now." He waved his gun towards me and Felicity. "These two, they'll be coming with us. The pig uniform'll look good."

We were taken downstairs. It seemed that the injured Korean was also to accompany the party, from which I deduced that the Stirling base had reached the end of its usefulness and was being abandoned, no-one at all being left behind. We were taken along the alley at the end of which, once again, a vehicle stood closely parked with the side door open to receive us. Again it was a minibus but not, this time, belonging to an oil company. It bore the name of a construction company and Kevin and his gunmen were wearing protective clothing – safety helmets and heavy cloth jackets, construction workers to the life. Deidre, I supposed, could have been the tea girl. She wasn't driving this time; a man, a new face, was behind the wheel and when he spoke to Kevin it was with a broad Scottish accent. Very good cover if stopped.

The Korean, in his semi-corpse-like state, was lifted in quickly and concealed beneath a blanket on the floor of the central aisle. Felicity and I were seated in the middle of the armed men, away from the doors. We had been given helmets like the others.

I heard Kevin say, as the vehicle moved off, "Maybe it'll work out in our favour. The evacuation. It'll scarcely have begun in any case."

Riley spoke then, viciously. "Begod, it better had! And somebody in bloody Derry's going to get what's coming to him."

I found that interesting; taken in conjunction with Seamus' reaction earlier, I sensed that indeed something had gone wrong and not just evacuation. What, I had no idea. But as the minibus negotiated the cobbles of that upward slope towards the castle I did begin to formulate a vaguish idea of what *might* have gone wrong. It began to look as though Kevin meant to enter the castle, running against the flow of the evacuation, assuming it was about to start – though I saw no sign of it yet. That, to my mind, meant one thing: the remote control set-up had gone off the beam and the job was to be done, somehow or other, from inside the castle itself.

Maybe the Derry men who were due for a lesson – knee-capping? – had been responsible for poor servicing of sophisticated equipment.

The minibus went on past the castle visitors' centre and reached the square outside the castle entry, a square used as a car park. The driver went on slowly for the drawbridge running over the dry moat, and we came between two big statues, one on the left being of a soldier of the 1914-18 War, a Highlander with rifle and full equipment, that on the right being of Robert the Bruce. Other vehicles were coming out and there was an air of urgency. Our driver was waved down to allow the egress, and a uniformed gatekeeper came out towards us from beyond the raised portcullis and big doors standing open.

The driver leaned from his window.

The gatekeeper said, "No vehicles allowed entry. We're clearing the castle." I saw him glance at my phoney police uniform.

The Scots driver said, "I have orders to go in to remove

168

some of the stuff from the chapel – "

"Orders? Who from, eh?"

"The boss. Colonel Anderson was onto him." There was a lull just then in the outcoming traffic. The driver took the chance to cross the narrow drawbridge, letting in his clutch and moving forward before the gatekeeper could stop him. The gatekeeper became somewhat embroiled with a traffic jam as another vehicle behind us, a private car driven by a young girl, tried to follow us and at the same time the outward traffic got on the move again. The minibus drove across the courtyard and stopped beneath a high, battlemented wall, alongside a sort of splinter-screen concealing an open door leading into what looked like a tunnel. Everyone got out; except for the Korean, who was left beneath his blanket. Felicity and I were pushed ahead of the guns, into the tunnel which was lit at intervals by overhead lights protected by metal bars like little cages. Two of the men had brought a suitcase out from the minibus. We moved along fast, deeper into the bowels of the castle as the tunnel took a downward slant. I believed we were not far off the section where Al Kufra had been held. In which case we were directly beneath the highest pinnacle of the castle, beneath the Argylls' mess with its commanding view across the historic battlefield of Bannockburn, the very heart of the castle.

We reached the tunnel's end. Blank stone. The man called Riley, the man of truth and destiny, got down on his hands and knees. The suitcase was passed along to him. He opened it. He brought out two reels of heavy insulated fuse-line. Then he ferreted around in the wall of the tunnel, first one side, then the other, while we watched.

"The plastic explosive," he said to Kevin. "Two thousand pounds all told. All the charges linked. It'll be a bloody bonfire of the Brits."

I saw the way it would go: all charges linked – right throughout the fabric of the castle probably, set by the IRA operators infiltrated into the work force. All to go up together when the fuse-lines, which Riley was now setting in place, were lit at the far end and burned down to the Semtex

169

explosive. It would be a bonfire right enough. Kevin asked anxiously, "How long will we have, Riley?"

Riley was engrossed in his task. I noticed that his hands were shaking a little. It was a tense moment for him, a moment approaching glory. He said, "From the time of lighting . . . just ten minutes. By that time we'll be away."

I put in a word about that. I said, "Not with the evacuating vehicles, you won't be. You'll be caught up in the line of traffic. Had you thought of that one, Riley?"

"Yes," he said. I thought: no, I can't shake you on that one. There was a back exit from the castle, a long slope down to the town, a track that emerged well clear of the castle rock and into a different part of the town far removed from the maze of cobbled streets and the buildings we had passed on the way in. Everything would have been well reconnoitred over many weeks. I believed it was unsuitable for vehicular traffic but a fast skedaddle on foot down that slope, and Riley and his friends would be well away, leaving total chaos and death behind them.

Riley, his work finished, stood up. The single eye gleamed with malevolence in the electric light overhead. "Move back now," he said to Kevin. "Take the reels with you."

A backward move started. We traversed the long tunnel towards its entry, the reels streaming out the fuse-line while we went along. Kevin was inclined to hurry; Riley said there was no rush. The ten minutes wouldn't start until he had ignited the fuse and that would give them plenty of time. Kevin asked about the Korean, still incapacitated in the minibus.

"We can't take him with us," Riley said impatiently, "and we don't want to leave him so as to put the finger on us – "

"So – "

"That's taken care of," Riley said. "Just in case the van survives the blast, blast being sometimes a funny thing." He laughed, a very unpleasant sound in that death-sown tunnel. Soon after that we reached the outward end. The exit door was shut; Riley had seen to that once we'd entered. Except for Kevin and Seamus the IRA contingent went through as Riley

170

opened the door. Then Riley blocked the way for Felicity and me with his gun.

"You stay," he said, grinning. While he bent and struck a match, putting it to the end of the fuse which he then led to the open air via the old-fashioned lock, Kevin and Seamus pinned us against the inside wall with their guns. It was an empty threat; they would never open fire at this stage of the game. I brought up a knee and got Seamus where it really hurt, and he doubled up in agony. Kevin lashed out with the barrel of his revolver, but I dodged aside in time and the metal struck the stone hard, doing no good to Kevin's wrist. It didn't do us any good either: Riley came in with a heavy fist that took me off guard and I crashed, bringing Felicity down with me.

There was a laugh from Riley and then the door shut and I heard bolts being shot across and the key turned in the lock. Then the lights went out: there must have been an outside switch. Scrabbling about in the dark I slipped and fell, and hit my head violently on the wall. I was just conscious of one happening before I passed out cold; a close and violent explosion that could, for all I was aware of then, have been something exploding in my own head.

I came round, so Felicity told me, fairly fast. I came round to the sound of her urgent voice. She was shaking me and she was panicking. She realised I was round when I lifted a hand to my head.

"The fuse-line! I don't know if it's burning or not, there's no smouldering! We have to – "

"There won't be any smouldering, Felicity. It burns along internally, inside its own casing. Otherwise they wouldn't have left us – "

"Can we pull it out, then?" She was crying, shaking life into me again. "Come on – hurry!"

I pulled myself together. I didn't see much hope. We ran along the tunnel, bouncing off the stone of the walls, making it as fast as we could. Felicity said I'd been out for about three minutes by guesswork. That, if she was right, left us just seven. We reached the end of the tunnel – I slammed right

171

into it in fact. I bent and scrabbled about for the fuse, running my fingers along it when I'd located it, along to where it fed into the rock and the Semtex.

I jerked at it. It didn't budge. Sweat was pouring off me now. I pulled and pulled. No result. Then something cut my hand quite badly, something on the ground. I felt for it. It was a stone, or a chip off the rock, fairly sizeable and with a very sharp edge. I went into a final attempt. I placed the sharp edge onto the fuse-line and started a sawing motion. No use; I hammered on the stone until my fist was raw and bleeding. Then the sharp edge at last did the trick. As the fuse-line parted, I smelt the stench of gunpowder and saw the red light of the smoulder at the end of the outward-leading fuse line in my hand. Just in time; and as the parted end of the fuse trail went out, I heard the pounding of running feet coming from the tunnel entry way behind us.

"All over," I said to Max on the line from Focal House. I'd been driven with Felicity to police HQ in Glasgow where I made the call. After giving Max the brief details I asked, "What about the Friends of Al Kufra?"

There was a grim laugh along the security line. "Spatchcock has had his way. A formula's been agreed for the release of the bastard. Links with Teheran, commercial links, remain intact. I suppose that's good."

"I suppose it is," I said, "for some. For Spatchcock. And the British economy. Not for those who've died. Not for the IRA either . . . not that I shed any tears over them." I added, "The Derry boys are largely dead. Blown to fragments." When we'd left the tunnel we'd seen the scattered wreckage of the mini-bus. Five of the IRA gunmen had been blown up with the North Korean, two were very badly injured. There had been a number of casualties, innocents caught in the blast, and there had been some structural damage, superficially, to the adjacent wall and buildings. I told Max all this.

"How come?" he asked.

I said, "Something went wrong, apparently. The bomb squad boys found . . . well, in layman's terms I'd call it

172

crossed wires in a fairly literal sense. The minibus was set to go up when Riley blew it from a portable radio link . . . explosives had been attached beneath the chassis. Very effective disposal of evidence. Anyway, that was where things went wrong. We don't know for sure how."

"This Riley – he set the minibus explosion off prematurely, I suppose?"

"By some cack-handedness, yes, probably. Similar things have happened before now. As we all know." I paused. "What about the rest of the Friends of Al Kufra?"

"Melted away," Max said briefly. "Part of the Spatchcock plan. They don't matter now and I'm not worried. At least we've got Behzad Habibi in custody. What are your plans, Shaw?"

I said, "I'll report in person if you want me to. But if you can spare me for a few days . . . convalescence, I aim to take a boat out on Loch Lomond."

Max's voice was sardonic. "With Miss Mandrake, I suppose?"

"Yes," I said.

He laughed. "Convalescence my backside," he said in a tone of assumed disgust. I left it at that, and took Felicity's hand as Max cut the call.